Burke

BENTLEY LEGACY BOOK 4

KATHI S. BARTON

World Castle Publishing, LLC
Pensacola, Florida
Copyright © Kathi S. Barton 2016
Paperback ISBN: 9781629893952
eBook ISBN: 9781629893969
First Edition World Castle Publishing, LLC, May 30, 2016
http://www.worldcastlepublishing.com

Licensing Notes

Cover: Karen Fuller
Editor: Eric Johnston
Editor: Maxine Bringenberg

Chapter 1

Burke stretched his neck and heard it pop twice before he leaned back in his chair. The ding of his computer, telling him he had an email, didn't even faze him. He was beyond exhausted, but as happy as he'd ever been in his life. He looked up when he felt someone in the room with him. Nolan smiled as he sat down across from him.

"What did he weigh?" Burke just slid the file over to him without moving much. "Wow, you were almost dead on. Nine pounds, ten and a half ounces. Christ, you might have hit the all-time record with this one."

"He was a bear to get free." Burke smiled again. "His daddy is about to bust his shirt, he is so proud. But I have a feeling that Momma is going to be saying no a lot more now that they have a son. Seven little girls and now a boy. I don't envy that little guy."

Burke had been worried for a bit when the baby had been breech. But the mom, a tiger, had told him to fix it. Burke did and then twelve minutes later, little Cartwright James had come into the world screaming his head off.

"You're settling in okay, right? I know it was hard for you at first." Burke nodded at Nolan and told him he thought he was. "When you came out of your office that first visit, I thought you were having a heart attack."

"I did too, to be honest. I wasn't used to people being so frank about why they were there. And then when he showed me his arm and told me that he'd cut it doing something so mundane as chopping wood on his farm, it was all I could do not to call the cops, thinking of foul play." Burke sat up in his chair when his computer dinged again. "I've been getting emails since Monday from the hospital. I've only read the first couple of them, but it looks like they're wanting me to come back at any cost. What do you suppose is going on?"

"I heard from Mom that there was a shake up about some of the surgeons. Something about a rotation schedule. To be honest, didn't really listen. What are they wanting you to do? Come back part time?" He told him what the one email said. "They want you to come back as chief of the hospital's emergency room? Wow, there really must be some shit going down. What are you going to tell them?"

"Nothing. I mean, as I said, I've not read more than a few of them, but even after the first one, I knew that I'd never go back. I love this job. I like what I'm doing. And I know that I've only been doing it for about a month, but I feel like I've found my dream job." Burke heard the computer again and turned off his speakers. "Mom told me that next week we're going over to her house for a little pre-Thanksgiving test tasting. I

6

have no idea what that even means."

"It means that she's going to try and cook up something strange and she wants us to approve it. I hate pre-whatever meals." Nolan stood up. "I have two more patients tonight, then I'm done. What about you?"

"I'm done. I have a few notes to make, but I have nothing to rush home for just now, and I thought I'd hang a few more things up. I finally got my things out of storage yesterday." Nolan nodded and told him not to be late tonight. "Nolan? Will you do me a favor? I'd like to find me a house. Nothing on the scale that you guys have, but something sedate and sort of smallish. Do you happen to know of a realtor, or someone selling?"

"We don't do smallish and sedate in this family. Haven't you learned that by now?" Burke was afraid he'd say that. "But it would be my pleasure. Do you have any ideas? Other than I'm assuming close to home?"

"Yes, close to home. I don't want to build. I have no desire to pick out carpets and wall shit. Just a house I can go to when I want to unwind, as well as a nice yard. Shane gave me a list, but I think the kid has it in his head that all of us Bentleys need giant homes. The two that he showed me were as big as your house."

Nolan laughed as he made his way out the door. But when he stopped and looked at him, Burke felt his cat run along his skin. "Are you happy, Burke? I don't mean with coming to work with me, but in general terms, are you happy?"

"I think so. I'm lonely most of the time. Not so much anymore because I can see the family more because I have a better schedule. Did you know that Walter has been popping over a lot? Well, he and Shane sometimes, too. And I'm telling you right now, that car you helped him buy has that kid thinking he's king of the world. And I guess he comes home from college a little more too since he got it." He knew he'd not answered his brother's question, not really, and changed the subject before he could ask him anything else. "I'll see you at Mom's at six for dinner. Then maybe we can go on a run if you and Rylee aren't too busy." Nolan told him it was a date.

When he was alone, Burke pulled out the boxes that he'd brought in on Monday. Then he got himself a bottle of water and his tool box. He smiled when he looked at the name that was engraved on the top. It had been his dad's, one that Burke had gotten for him when he'd been about ten. Running his fingers over the crooked letters that spelled out Dad, he thought of his father again.

Burke and his father had been close. Not as close as he and Micah had been, but almost. His dad, Grandda, and he would meet up once a week to go fishing, even if his dad had to miss a little overtime to do it. It had become their time. Then one day, it had only been him and his grandda.

"He loved you." Burke told Grandda that he knew that. Burke's father had been killed a couple of years before, right around Thanksgiving. This time of year as a matter of fact. "Didn't think I'd outlive him, never dreamed of it. And here I am, sitting with my grandson, feeling both our grief overwhelming us."

"Grandda, I think he knew that he was going to die." His grandda had nodded but said nothing as they both sat there with their poles forgotten in the water. "He told me that if I did nothing else in life, that I should be happy. No matter if I wanted to be a homeless man. Just so long as I did something that made me feel good and happy."

"He sure did love what he did." Burke knew that as well. "My boy Micah told me once that being a cop like I had been was one of his greatest pleasures in life, besides marrying your momma and having you boys. I wish all the time that he'd not been killed and that he was right here with us. I worry about your momma too."

"She's really sad. And I hear her crying all the time too." Grandda had nodded and blew his nose in his handkerchief. "I don't think she wants to live anymore. Her heart is just too broken."

"No, but she will. Now she will."

Burke had heard them talking. Mom was telling his grandma and grandda that she wasn't fit to be their momma anymore. She didn't have it in her to want to go on. Grandma had sobbed hard, and Grandda got mad at her. Burke wasn't sure what had happened after that. He'd been called away by one of his brothers.

And she had gotten better after that. Flourished even more since the grandchildren had come along, as well as the three wives of his brothers. Burke took out the first framed picture and smiled. It was the one they'd taken at the charity event last month, all of them standing in their finest and happy. There were others of them as a family…the babies, as well as Shane, were in them. But this one, the one taken of them sitting at the table all together and smiling when someone asked them to turn to them…Burke thought it was his favorite.

Burke was just putting the nail in the wall for the last framed picture when there was a knock at the door. Telling his assistant, Margaret, to come in, he turned to her when she didn't speak. The man at the door with a knife to Margaret's throat had him reaching for not just Micah, but all of his family to tell them what was going on.

You know him? He told Garth that he did not. *We're coming. I'm with Tony, and Micah and Reggie are close too.*

The man started talking to him, using Margaret as his shield. "You go over there." Burke did what he was told and moved with his hands up. "Where is she? I want you to bring her right on out here now."

"Her who?" When he hit Margaret with the knife butt, Burke felt his cat run along his skin. "I'm trying to be helpful here, but I don't know who you might be talking about. And that being said, I can't bring her without that information."

"Captain McClure. I want her now." It took him several seconds to remember who he was talking about. Rylee, Nolan's wife. "You tell her that she needs to come and see what she's done to me."

"All right. I'll do that for you if you let Margaret go. She's done nothing to you." He told Nolan what was going on and he asked for the man's name. "You just tell me who you are and I'll call her right now. No funny business."

"You fucking damn well right there won't be no funny business. I want her here, and if you think I'm giving over this woman, then you're stupider than them bastards at the hospital." He told Nolan what he'd said. "My name is Franklin. They won't treat me no more."

"What is it you need treating for, Mr. Franklin?" He told him that his first name was Franklin. "All right then, Franklin, what is it that you need treatment for?"

"I got me a wound." Burke nodded as he made his way to his desk. There was nothing there that he could use against a knife, but he was going to be calm and cool about this. "They said that it's not nothing they did, so they ain't gonna help me out."

"Can I look at it? I'm not sure what you thought that McClure could help you with, but I'm a doctor." He nodded and held the knife tighter to Margaret's throat. "You hurt her and I won't have anyone to help me treat you. And I won't, either, if you don't let her go."

"She said that we could get fixed up. But that guy down there said no. He said that it wasn't related to the army." Burke asked him what place he'd gone. "Down to the new place that has been helping us out. You know, the Micah Bentley place."

"Yes, I know the place. I work there, as well as one of my brothers. He's the one that started it." Franklin looked as if he didn't believe him. "Nolan, he's my brother and a good doctor too. He did that for you. And if someone turned you away, I'll find out why for you."

"I hurt." Burke nodded and moved a little closer. Franklin was looking weaker now, his face pale. Burke could feel something wrong with him but not what. It wasn't until he felt Chris touch his mind that he knew.

He has something on his spine, a cut along with a few other injuries. He had to escape. But to be honest, I don't know what that means. His mind is all jumbled up. They won't treat him because he's got other issues. Mostly that his mind is hurting. They thought him too depressed to help. But the doctor there is being dealt with as we speak. Your mom is there at the clinic now. Burke could almost feel sorry for whoever it had been. *Your brothers are nearly there, but I've told everyone to wait. You have this under control, don't you, Burke?*

He told her he hoped so, but to send in Rylee if that was okay with Nolan. The man was a human, and he might not know that he was a panther. Instead of pretending to use the phone, he told him that he'd contacted his brother.

"I want McClure here. She told me I'd be all right." He told him how he was related to her. "Oh. Then she's coming here?"

"Yes, but I won't let her come in here until you let Margaret go. You're scaring her, and I really like her. I need her to work with me." Franklin said he was right sorry. "I know you are. Just let her go and I'll have a look at your back. Then when Rylee gets here, you can talk to her."

He staggered back from Margaret, who turned and slapped Franklin. When he just stood there, his face looking sort of sad, Burke asked her to set up a room for them. She nodded once and started out of the room.

"You do something like that to me again, Franklin, and you will think that Rylee is sweet on you when I'm finished with your old body." Franklin looked at him when Margaret left the room. "Rylee is on her way."

"I think that nurse is mad at me." Burke nodded. "I want you to know that I only came here on account'a I knew the Captain was here sometimes. I heard tell that she hangs out here. Guess nobody knew that she had herself a husband that worked here too."

"She's married to my brother, Nolan." He knew he was repeating himself, but Burke was trying to get his thoughts together. When Margaret came back to say that Rylee was here, Burke put out his hand. "I want the knife. And any other weapon you have on you. I'll not have you trying to hurt her when's she's done us both a favor."

"I like her." Burke said he did as well. And when he put the knife in his hand, he asked him if there was more. "They took it from me when I went to the hospital once. Said I was unfit to carry any more. I was fit to carry when I had a bullet in me and they was needing me overseas, but now that I need to get some help, I'm unfit."

"You come on along then and we'll work on this." He saw Rylee just as he was guiding Franklin into the room. He asked for one minute and she nodded. Burke went in and saw that Margaret had gotten his shirt off already. Burke wasn't prepared for what he saw on the man.

~~~

Pip searched up and down the long building, trying her best not to cry. Franklin had been missing for four days now, and she was sure that he'd been arrested again or murdered. When the young man who had been trying to keep up with her finally did, she asked him again if he'd heard that he was here.

"His name isn't on the list, miss. You said he could write, and he's just not there." She'd been confused by that when he'd asked her if he could write his name. He explained that there were plenty of men there that could not. "Mrs. Bentley is with the doctors now or I'd ask them if they — miss, you can't go in there."

She'd seen the room earlier where a bunch of people were closed off in a room. Pip knew they were mostly doctors and other staff. Why they were having a meeting now was sort of mind boggling to her since there were people everywhere that needed help. But she was missing the only man she'd ever loved, and one of them had to know where he was.

The door opened easily. She'd been sure it would have been locked. And when she walked in, she almost had the feeling that they were expecting her. Which wasn't possible, as she'd only just gotten into town. A woman sitting at the head of the table was laughing, but the older woman who looked to be in charge just stared.

"I'm trying to find out if my uncle has been here. I heard from someone at the VA that he'd been...well, he escaped. They're not very good at keeping him safe, and I've tried my best to get them to understand that he hates to be tied down, but they don't listen. I've had to take on two jobs as well as move here to try and get him to be signed over to me." She looked around the room. "I've shared too much. But I need to find him."

"What's his name?" She told the older woman. "Ah. We were just talking about him. Come on in, dear, and have a seat. And so you know, we know just where he is and he's in good hands."

"I want to go to him. Now if you don't mind." The woman nodded but didn't move. "Perhaps you didn't get it. I want to go get him and take care of him. Wherever he is, it can't be safer than when he's with me."

"He's with my son, Burke, who is taking care of him. He broke into Burke's offices and demanded to see a woman by the name of Captain McClure. That would be my daughter-in-law, Rylee." She asked what this man was doing for him. "He's a doctor. Burke said that he's doing some minor surgery on him now, and that he'd have him brought here in about thirty minutes."

Before she could think that she was light headed, she was sitting in a chair with her head between her knees. The shoes in front of her were expensive and looked comfortable. For a moment she wondered what it would cost to have something like that, and heard someone laugh. Pushing against the hand that held her, she looked at the face of the younger woman that had been seated.

"You all right now?" Pip nodded. "Here, you drink this juice and I'll tell you what I know. Franklin Bradshaw was here earlier today. And yesterday, from what we've been able to piece together. He was turned away both times." Pip emptied the tall glass of orange juice and realized it was fresh with pulp, the best kind.

"Why? I mean, you have your doors open for anyone, correct? Not that he should have been out and about on his own, but I thought this place was for people like him, vets."

The woman nodded. "I'm Piper Cordale, everyone just calls me Pip."

"Chris Bentley." Pip looked around then back at the woman. "Yes, my family owns and runs this place. That's why we're taking care that your uncle gets the best care now and that the people who turned him away are dealt with. Not everyone is cut out for helping the lost."

"I've been trying to help him, but he's a lot to handle. I suppose he'd say the same thing about me." Chris nodded. "And you should know that I'm not his niece but his friend. For some reason it's easier to get someone to listen to me when I say that I'm related to him. Franklin hasn't anyone left, and I've been trying to make things easier for him."

"At what cost to you?" Pip said nothing but played with the condensation on the now full glass. "Does he know what you are?"

"No. I don't think so. I mean, he might have at one time, but his mind is a little fuzzy at time on details." Chris said nothing. "That other woman, she said that her son was working on him. Can you tell me what happened to him?"

"He was injured when he tried to get away from the hospital. Burke said that in addition to the wound at his back, he also had bruising around his wrists and ankles. He said it looked to him like they tied him down." She said they had to at times to keep him from hurting himself. "No, that's not why they do it and you know it. It's why you're trying to get him to come live with you. Please don't lie to me, Pip. We won't have a good relationship if you do."

Pip looked at her. "I'm not sure what you mean by that, but I really don't think we're going to be best of buds, do you? I mean, you know as well as I do that I'm broke." Chris cocked a brow at her. "Yes, I know what you are and who you are. And

I'm also pretty sure you can read my mind. Not that I have much in the way of secrets. But if you want to know something then don't rape my mind. Ask me."

"All right. And the only thing that I got from your head was about my shoes. By the way, they're very comfortable. When I touched you, all your emotions came to me and I can't stop those. Also, I wanted to make sure that you were all right as well." Pip nodded. "You're not, are you? All right, I mean."

"No. I have issues as well. Chronic Major Depression, or CMD as my file says on it. It's what brought the two of us together all those years ago." Chris asked her how. "I was ready to jump. I had no idea he was there as well, on the building I mean. And when I lifted my hands off the railing that I'd been holding onto, he grabbed me from behind. No matter how much I fought him to be let go, he hung onto me like it was his business. I wasn't able to shake him for another year and a half."

"But that didn't stop you, did it?" Pip pulled her sleeves down over her wrists and said nothing. "Franklin told Nolan that you were his niece just now. He asked me to have you be there when they come in."

"Is he going to be all right?" Chris said that he was now. "I need him in my life as much as he does me, I guess. If anything were to happen to him.... I just don't want anything to happen to him, that's all."

"Is it what you are that has you so depressed?" Pip just shrugged as she emptied the glass of juice again, only to have it full when she sat it on the table. "If you want something different, I can get it for you."

"Cranberry." The glass, which had been full of orange juice, was now filled with a dark red, blood like juice. Picking it up, Pip moaned as the flavor and the richness rolled over her tongue. Almost as soon as she set the glass down, it was full again. "Thank you."

"You could have done it on your own." Pip just shook her head. The depression, coming in waves more and more lately, nearly had her falling to the floor. But a touch from Chris and she could feel it dissipate. Not leave her; there was only one way for that to happen, but it did lessen a little. "How long have you been off your meds?"

"Five years, six months, and twenty-nine days. Since I lost my insurance, along with my job, when I couldn't function at work when they fucked with my dosage. It happens at times. The place where I got my medications wasn't the best of places, and I don't think they got the dosages just right when I picked them up. It had happened before." Pip smiled at Chris. "I guess it's what you are that makes it so I can't lie to you."

"No, you don't want to lie to me." Chris stood, and so did Pip. "They're here. Nolan, my brother-in-law, is with Burke and would like for you to hang back a little until they get Franklin in a room. He's afraid that if you show, he'll get upset again." Pip nodded. "Rylee is with Franklin as well. He knows her from the service."

"His boss, I guess." Pip sat down again when Chris told her she'd be back. The glass filled when she'd emptied it again. She was going to be buzzing soon if she didn't stop. But as a faerie that hadn't had any for a while, she was getting it while the getting was good. And she had a feeling that despite what Chris had hinted at earlier, she'd not be seeing the grand witch again.

Chapter 2

Howie was sitting in his office when he saw Shane walk by his door. He'd not known that his grandson was around and got up to see what he was about. He was just going to see if he wanted to go out in the woods for a nice walk when he heard him talking. Howie waited.

"But I know she won't let me. She'll say I'm too young, and really, I think I am." Howie wanted to know what was going on now more than ever. "Yeah, I know, but I'm not going to go there when I know she's not going to say yes. And my dad will murder me. Then there will be a line of them to want to yell at me for doing something stupid like this."

After he told the person on the other end he was hanging up, Howie stepped into the hall and said his name. Shane looked about as guilty as a kid could get. Howie invited his grandson into his domain.

"I guess you know." Howie thought it best if he played along and nodded. "I told some of my friends I wasn't going to go to this party. It's not right that these kids think that just because their parents are gone that it's okay to mess up the house and stuff."

"But?" Shane got up to pace and didn't say anything. Howie would have to figure out who was leaving town and nip the party in the bud somehow. "You thinking that you might go on ahead or something? I'm telling you right now, that ain't gonna set well with me. And it especially won't with your momma and dad."

Nothing. Howie was thinking that this was beyond his realm when Shane looked at him. He could see fear there, a lot of it, and it worried him something powerful. Standing up, he walked slowly to the boy, not wanting him to bolt. He looked like a rabbit just out of his hole.

"There's this girl." Howie nodded, not sure where he was going. "They make fun of her, these two boys and their friends. They're brothers, and one of them is just as mean as a snake. The other one, he's not so bad when he's not with his brother. If I don't go, I'm afraid that they're going to do things to her when she gets there. Nasty things."

"I see. You and this girl, you friends?" Shane said that he didn't have many friends, but she talked to him. "Why is that? You're a good boy. You're a Bentley, ain't you?"

"Yes. But I don't know how to be like them. And usually, I don't want to be." Howie asked him what that was supposed to mean. "I've never been rich like them, and I don't know how to be like they are. You know, sort of uncaring of anyone but people like them. The rich and the famous kind of people."

"You don't have to be like nobody but you. And them boys, they're from families that think they are better than you because of this?" Shane nodded. "I see. And this girl, she older or younger than you? I'm asking because while I want to know, I won't ask you to rat anyone out."

"I don't mind, because they're going to hurt her, I know it. They're the Mason twins, Billy and Carter. Their parents are the ones that donate tons of money to the hospital." Howie knew them, the entire pain in the ass family of them. "I know that we have money, more than me and Aunt Rylee...Mom ever had in all my life. But these guys, they act like because I'm not old money, I'm not money at all. I don't understand what the difference is. And even if I did, what does it matter?"

"None that I can think of right now. And so you know, you come from older money than they do. My pappy's pappy had money before them people even knew what the meaning of being rich is. We just don't exploit people to get them to do what we want because of it." Howie wasn't really sure how to go about this. He knew that Shane's parents would have to know before too long, but he wanted something done. "I'm gonna tell your grandma and great-grandma. I think we might be in over our heads, don't you think?"

"Grandma will be upset with me for even thinking about going on without telling anyone." He assured him that she'd be a lot more upset with him if he didn't do nothing. "Okay, but I have to tell you, I'm not liking that you're going to get me in a world of hurt."

"I'm not liking it either. But you ain't done nothing wrong but come to an old man about something bothering you, right?" Shane seemed to mull that over and Howie just about laughed. He looked so much like Nolan that he'd swear that they were blood related. "I'm gonna call them in now. You just tell them like you told me. And I swear to you, I won't let them get their dander up."

He wasn't sure how he was going to do that, but he'd sure try. Calling his mate in, Katie came in with Gracie and he felt like he might need some back up. He loved them both to death and beyond, but he was terrified of both of them. Howie nearly fell to his knees when Micah came in too.

An hour later, without a single loud voice coming into it, Shane was in on the plan. It was a good one, if he did say so himself. They were going to tell the parents of both the girl and the boys. Howie was thrilled to death that the love of his life, along with his daughter-in-law and grandson, told the youngster how great it was that he came to them with this. Micah even shook Shane's hand, telling him he was proud of him for being a man about this issue.

"There is no telling what they might have done to her." Shane looked at him, then at the floor. Howie knew then that he knew just what they had planned. He'd not thought to ask him directly. "What is it, Shane? What are they going to do to that poor girl?"

"She's pretty and all." Micah nodded. "And she has...she's got...she's a girl and it shows." It took Howie a bit longer than it did the rest of them, but he felt his own face heat up. The kid meant she had breasts. He wondered when he'd figure out they weren't nothing to be embarrassed about. Too soon, Howie figured.

"Was what they were going to do with her sexual?" Shane nodded at Micah, still looking at the floor. "Shane, look at me and tell me what they were planning to do with this young woman." The look of fear on his face made Howie want to go to Shane and tell Micah to back off. But this was important. Not just to the girl, but for Shane as well. He had to learn to be able to come to them, no matter the issue at hand.

"They got this drug off their father. Mr. Mason uses it

sometimes when he has a girl that won't put out at his office. Billy said that his daddy called it his miracle...fuck." He whispered the last word, but they could all hear it. "I had to go and look it up to figure out what he meant. Anyway, he gave one of them to Billy to...sheesh, Uncle Micah, this sure is hard. But he wanted to let Billy and Carter get their cherry popped with this girl."

Howie covered his mouth. He wasn't sure what was going to spill from his lips, but he was sure it was going to get him into a lot of trouble with his mate if he let go of his temper. Mr. Mason was drugging his employees to get laid, and he was encouraging his own son to do it too? What the heck was this world coming to?

"This changes everything, Shane. You know that, don't you?" Shane nodded at Micah. "They were going to rape this girl, drug her and rape her. And if Grandda hadn't heard you on the phone, then they would have gotten by with it."

"I wasn't talking to anyone. I mean, I could have been, but I wasn't." No one said a word. "I knew he was in there. I'd been waiting all morning for his door to be open so I could pretend to talk to somebody so he'd ask me about it. I was trying to...I didn't know what to do. They didn't invite me so I wasn't sure how to save her. I'm sorry I lied to you, Great-Grandda, but I was too...I've never even talked to my parents about sex, and I knew you'd help me with that too."

Howie looked at Micah, who looked like someone had hit him right between the eyes. Then when Gracie started laughing, it was all he could do not to get up and see if she was fevered. He wasn't sure what was going on when his own mate started laughing with her. He and Micah just stared at them.

"He played you. Quite nicely too." He asked Katie what she meant. "Oh, I'm not saying that this lessens the fact that

Carl Mason is going to pay for this, but you have to admit, Shane did this brilliantly. He got what he wanted and didn't have to do anything more than to let you eavesdrop on his conversation with himself. You should be proud of him. He acts just like you do."

"But he lied." Gracie told Micah that Shane had done no such thing. "He told Grandda that he was talking to someone."

"No, all he did was say that he knew this girl was in trouble. He never said that he was actually talking to anyone." Howie still felt like he'd been wronged somehow. Then Shane came to him.

"I wasn't sure how to come in here and say, 'Great-Grandda, I know these boys who are gonna do something very bad to this girl.'" He looked around the room, then back at him. "I knew in my heart that I could do it, come in here. But I was afraid that...I've never had anyone that I could talk to before, and I wasn't sure how to start it up."

"You just start it." Shane nodded and said he knew that now. "And so you know, if my door is ever closed, you can knock on it and I can tell you to come on in if I can talk to you. Even if I can't right then, I'll come find you when I got the time. You got that?"

"Yes, sir." Shane asked for a hug and Howie could not have turned him away if he'd wanted too. Holding the little boy to his body, it was like he'd hugged his heart, too. "I know that I've done this all wrong. But I knew that if anyone could get it taken care of, you could. No problem. And if you couldn't, you'd do just what you did and call in people that could help us."

Howie pulled the boy into his arms and held him again. Damn, but he thought he couldn't have loved him any more than he did at that moment. If it wasn't so dad-burned cold out, he'd take him to the dock to drown a worm or two.

After calling in Shane's parents and Chris to tell them how to go about this, things got heated. But through it all, Shane never left his side. The boy had impressed him now that he'd had time to think of his planning. He was just like him in that department, he decided. Working the house to do what you want. Yes, sir, when the weather broke, they were gonna get them a boat and go out fishing.

~~~

Pip held Franklin's hand and watched him sleep. He'd been brought in over an hour ago, and once they got him settled, he'd been given something more for pain. She cried every time he moved and moaned in pain. Those bastards were going to pay this time. Laying her head down on his hand as she held him, she told him what she was going to do.

"There's this house over on Tenth. I think that's the number. Anyway, it had three bedrooms and a pretty good-sized tub for you to take your weekly baths in." She grinned at him. "I'll see about getting you some of that manly bubble bath you like so much. It's not too far from the downtown area, so we can walk around and get the stuff we need for food. And hopefully I can find me a job so I can pay for the rent."

Pip had put her application in at three different places yesterday and hadn't heard anything back from them. If they didn't call her by Friday, she was going to be shit out of luck on a lot of things. Her phone was set to be shut off. She could make arrangements to pay it, they told her, but without work, there was no point in that either.

"I met some really nice people today. I think you'd like them. They're going to look into why you were hurt in the first place, and why they didn't report you missing. Had I not.... Well, it matters little now. You're safe and we might be able to get this behind us soon enough." Pip closed her eyes. It had been so long since she'd had a place to rest, she knew that she was going to crash soon if she didn't. "Franklin, I really wish every day that you had just let me go. I know that you think I've saved you a few times as well, but I really didn't want to be saved. And anyone will help you."

"Why don't you think anyone would save you?" She lifted her head and looked at the man standing there. He was big and a shifter, a panther. She wondered for a moment if he was related to the other woman and let his scent come to her. He had been with the grand witch recently was all she could tell from this distance. "You didn't answer my question."

"I don't know if you are aware of this or not, but it's really rude to walk in on a conversation that has nothing to do with you and expect someone to tell you all about it." He came into the room and sat in the chair across from her and the bed. "Did you need something? Are you lost, perhaps?"

"Yes. No." Pip wasn't sure what he was answering her for and he smiled. It was one that would melt even the coldest of hearts, she'd bet. "Yes, I need something. A great deal I think. And no, I'm not lost. I know just where I'm supposed to be."

"Well, good for you." He nodded and stretched out his long legs in front of him. "I think you should go now. I'm keeping an eye on my uncle in the event that he wakes and get frightened again."

"He's been given something that should let him rest all night. I didn't want him to pull out the stitches that I put in." He was Burke Bentley. The doctor. He closed his eyes as he leaned his head back on the seat. "You're a faerie. I might not have guessed that, but Chris told me. She said that you were having some issues."

"I'm just fine." He nodded but didn't look at her. "Look, I

thank you for fixing him up, but I'd really like to be left alone."

"You're my mate." He hadn't moved, not even to look at her since he'd put his head back. "I wasn't sure at first when I smelled your scent on Mr. Bradshaw, but once I came in here, I knew. I'm Burke Bentley, in case you didn't know that."

"I know who you are. And I believe you're mistaken. My scent isn't one you can smell. Because of what I am." He nodded, then yawned. It took a great deal of effort for her not to yawn as well. "Don't you have a bed or something you can go to?"

He lifted his head and looked at her. "Will you join me in it? We could both use a really good nap, I think. Then we could make love all night. Would you like that?"

"No." He smiled and put his head back down and told her too bad. "I'm not sure why you think that pulling this shit on me is funny, but I'd really like for you to go away."

"I can't. I have to be where you are." If she'd been standing and closer to him, she might have hit him. "As for your scent, Chris told me that you would be able to hide your scent from anyone but me. Your mate. But I can most assuredly smell you. You smell of flowers and honey. Do you suppose your entire body smells that way? I told Chris the scents that I could smell on Franklin here, and she said that makes you an earth faerie. There aren't too many of you around, she also said."

"I'm aware of that too." She laid her head back down on Franklin's hand. There had to be a reason for him telling her this load of shit. Maybe he knew what she was worth on the market. A vampire told her once that she was priceless to his kind…right before she killed him. Closing her eyes, she thought of that bastard.

He'd wanted to take her back to his lair and have a party. She was going to be the guest of honor; also the main course.

She was glad when he'd tried to take her to his dungeon that she'd at least had the heads up to know what he was going to try to do to her. Shoving her magic into his chest had worked better than any stake in his body would have done. There wasn't even ash to clean up.

"There is something that I think you should know before you go much further in your memories. I can read your mind. I wouldn't have to if you talked to me, but there you have it." She sat up and looked at him. She was going to have to kill the man, she knew it. "You can't hurt me either. I hope not anyway. But I would like to have a conversation with you sometime about this vampire and his ideas on what he thought you were going to do for him."

"He's dead, what does it matter to you?" He sat up then. Burke was a big man, even sitting she could tell that he was. He frightened her enough that she could feel her bit of magic race over her fingers. "Are you willing to take the chance that I can't hurt you?"

"No. And yes. I'd like very much to touch you right now. Run my fingers through your hair to see if it is as soft and silky as it looks. Taste your mouth. I have a feeling that it's warm, despite the fact that you want to be cold to me." He stood up and made his way to her. "If I hold you to my body, are you going to fit as well as I hope? Will your breasts fill my hands as well as my mouth when I suckle at them? I was thinking also whether or not you would scream when you came. Would you bite me when I marked you as my own?"

"Don't come any closer." Her magic danced along her skin now. She was aroused and she was pretty sure that Burke knew it. "You can't smell me. It's what makes it so I can't be captured. Tell me who told you. Was it Chris? She'd be the only one that would know what I smell like."

"I can smell you and you know why." She backed up when he took a step toward her. "You also know that as my mate, there is no way for us to stay apart. Not now that we've found each other."

"I don't have to do shit with you." He nodded but took another step toward her. "I've asked you not to come any closer. I would really like it if you stopped it. I can't think."

"All right. But you're not leaving.... I would very much like it if you didn't leave here without telling me. I want to talk to you." She asked him what he thought they had to talk about. "What we're going to do now that we've found each other. How you want to proceed."

"I don't want to proceed with anything. I'm having a hard enough time just keeping myself from wanting to end my life every minute of every day." He asked her why. "Because I hate breathing. Feeling my heart beat in my chest. I don't care for the way others look at me, as if I'm faking what I'm feeling. Or that they think I can just fix it."

"You suffer from CMD, Chris told me. But I can also feel it in your mind and heart. I know that I can't understand completely what you're going through, but I would like to help." She shook her head at him. "I want to help, love. Even as a doctor I know there isn't any way that I can understand fully how you're feeling. But I do know that when you have support, it makes it feel less overwhelming."

"Do you now? Well good for you. You know that I feel like I'm wrapped up in a thick blanket of blackness. That every part of my body hurts from forcing myself to move. Breathe in and out. To know that if my heart would just cooperate and stop beating I'd be at peace." He touched her then, his hands gently at each of her shoulders. "Let me go. I don't need this any more than you do."

His body fit hers. She had no idea why that felt so important to her, but she liked it. And when he pulled her closer, his body leaning into hers, it was all Pip could do not to grab him, hold him as tightly as she wanted. Then he lifted her chin up, looked down at her face, and she could see his compassion. She knew that he might on some level care about how she was dealing with this.

"You don't have to fight this alone." She nodded. "No, you don't. I can help you stay steady, if you'll let me. I want to help you keep breathing, your heart to beat. Please, just lean on me."

It was too much. All the wishing for him to leave her just went out the door when he kissed her forehead and told her that he was there for her. Pip cried, sobbed hard at the feeling of having someone, even for this brief period of time, to lift her up, hold her in a way that no one had ever bothered to do for her before.

She had no idea how long he held her, or at what point he'd picked her up in his arms and sat in the chair with her on his lap. He spoke to her, softly and gently, telling her of things that he'd do for her if she'd let him. Things that Pip had been told before.

"You have to trust me. I know that we know very little about each other, but I promise you, I'm going to help you." She told him she didn't have to do anything. "True, but I'd like for you to trust me. Even for now. So I can prove to you that I'm really going to be here for you."

"I don't want you to be here for me, don't you see that? I just want to be left alone." He nodded. "Why are you being nice to me? And if you say that you have to, then I still won't believe you. There isn't any possible way for you to know that I'm anything to you. She put you up to this, didn't she? Chris said that we were something that she wanted to happen and put it in your head."

"Do you know what Chris is?" She said that didn't mean anything. "No, not really, but she has a little insight that we don't. Not even us who know her as well as we do. But when I asked her about the scent, she told me that you and I were mates and that you were in here. She never told me anything else but that you were caring for my patient. I'm not even sure what your name is."

"Piper Cordale. But I go by Pip." She tried to stand up, but he held her to him. "Let me go please. This is not solving anything."

"Isn't it?" He tilted her head so that he could look into her eyes. "You're the most beautiful creature I've ever seen. May I please kiss you, Piper?"

Chapter 3

Burke was sure she was going to turn him down. So instead of waiting for her answer, he leaned down and pressed his lips to her. When she didn't bite him or harm him in anyway, he deepened the kiss by sliding his tongue over her mouth and gaining access to her richness. And rich she was.

She tasted of honeysuckle and honey, as he'd thought before. Turning her body so that she was in front of him, he felt her warmth, her full breasts against his chest. Cupping her ass, he brought her closer to him, moaning when she rolled her hips, and held her tighter still just to feel her heat. When he lifted his head from hers, he stared down at her and saw the changes in her.

"Your eyes are greener than before. Your hair is lighter, almost white." She nodded. "What else has evolved with you? Please, I want to see it."

Her wings spread out from behind her. They were light, like her hair, colored with sparks of green that were as beautiful as her eyes. And when she moved, he saw that her skin had changed as well, and it too sparkled in the light, like tiny stars danced along her skin. And when she wrapped her legs around his hips, Burke was sure that he was going to come in his pants and wondered how disappointed she'd be.

"I'm an earth faerie, like you were told. But I'm not very strong." He asked her why not, having a hard time concentrating on much more than her hips rocking to meet his. "I have no mate. And even if I did, I haven't had much in the way of practice with my magic. I'd just as soon leave it where it is. People...they would hurt me for it."

He lifted her up, careful not to wake the man in the bed in front of him. Moving with her to the bathroom, then sitting her on the counter, he closed the door behind them. Taking her mouth again, touching her wherever he could with his hands, he made short work of her blouse. The need to taste her was hurting him.

"I want you." Instead of telling him no again, she helped him to pull his shirt over his head. "Christ, I need to be deep inside of you. I want to drink from you as well. Lick your pussy until you flood my mouth with your cream."

The pounding at the door had him snarling at it. "Burke, I'm really sorry, but we have an emergency out here. I need you."

"I can't." Tony said he had to and told him again how sorry he was. "Anthony, I swear to Christ if you don't go away I'm going to—"

"Mom's been hurt." Burke knew that he needed to go. But he was also torn about leaving Piper. She would run, he had no idea why he knew that, but he was sure that she would as soon as he was gone. "Are you coming out?"

"Yes, now. I have to…give me a second." He pulled his shirt back on and reached for her blouse to help her. When she slapped his hands away, he took a step back from her. "I have to go."

She nodded, and he wanted to scream out his frustrations. Not for not having her, but because he was hurting her and he knew it. When he went to the door, he turned back to her.

"Don't leave me. Please? I beg of you not to leave me." She said nothing, didn't even look at him. "Piper? Will you wait for me?"

"I have to see to Franklin. Go to your mom, and I'd like for you to leave me alone." He had no time to argue with her, as Micah was in his head telling him to hurry. As soon as he left Piper, Burke had a feeling it was going to be hard for him to find her again.

Mom had been hit by a car. While she could heal herself when she was hurt, it wouldn't work if she was unconscious. And she was losing a great deal of blood too. As he worked with Tony to try and stem the blood flow, he thought of all the things that he had to do to keep her alive. Piper was there, just in the background of his thoughts, but this was first and foremost in his mind.

Doing what came as natural to him as breathing, he inventoried each of her injuries. Left leg broken in two places. Right arm shattered. Lacerations to face and neck, but nothing life threatening there. It was the wound at her belly that had him scared. She had a large piece of glass still protruding from her.

"We need to get her to surgery, right? She needs to have this taken out." He nodded at Tony. "Then what? Tell me, Burke, then what do we do?"

"We have to remove the glass. Once that is out, we can stitch her up until she can shift. If she loses much more blood, she won't make it, but it won't come to that." Tony nodded and he could hear his grandma crying behind him. "Right now we have to get her set to move. The leg and arm are going to need to be set, but they aren't as important as this bleeding wound is at the moment. Where is Nolan?"

"I'm here." He dropped down beside him and helped him to stabilize their mom. After a few minutes, though it seemed like years, they were ready to take her in. When she screamed when they picked her up, both of them stopped moving. Burke hurt when his mom did. And as soon as she was settled again, he nodded to his brother.

"Go." They moved inside and were rushing her down the long hall to the surgery. Just as they were ready to wheel her into the sterile room, Nolan stopped moving. Burke's focus had been on his mom, and when Nolan stopped, he looked up to tell him to get going and saw Piper there.

"I can save her." Everyone looked at Burke when she did. "It will cost me, but I can do it. With your help. If you're what you say you are to me, then we can save her. It's her only hope and you all know it."

"What do you need for me to do?" She shook her head at Nolan and moved to the gurney. "Piper, what is it you need me to do?"

"Just remove the glass when I tell you to." She was crying and he wanted to ask her what was wrong, but she spoke again. "As soon as the glass is gone, Burke, you'll have to touch me. Just my skin. That's all. Being my mate, you'll lend me some of what you are. You're going to be as weak as a kitten when we're done."

Nolan and Micah put their hands on the glass. Piper stood

on the opposite side of them and the gurney. At her nod, the glass was torn from their mom's belly, and the scream this time was painful for them, even their cats felt it. As soon as Piper put her hand on his mom's wound, he touched his fingers to her arms and felt it.

Power surged from her. Not just from her hands, but everywhere. And when her wings unfolded, Burke heard someone say "Holee-shit" and knew it was his grandda. Almost as soon as he touched his hands over her arms, the bleeding stopped and his mom's blouse started to clear up too. As he watched, he noticed that her blood, his mom's blood, was seeping back into the wound that was as bright now as Piper. As soon as Mom took a deep breath and opened her eyes, Piper fell back. It was all he could do to catch her.

The stain on her own blouse deepened. The red of blood scared him and he started to put his hands over it. Chris stopped him, told him to watch as her body lifted from his arms by an unseen force and then settled down again. And as quickly as the blood flow on her had started, it disappeared just as it had done on his mom.

"Take her to a room and stay with her." He nodded but was unable to move. It wasn't until Micah hit him in the head that he seemed to understand. Chris spoke to him again. "You have to take her somewhere she can rest. Find a room and put her in it."

"Yes, all right." He held her to him and felt lost. It wasn't until he looked at his mom that he knew what she'd done. Not only had Piper healed her, but she more than likely had saved her life. He was sure of it. "Mom? Are you all right?"

"Yes." She nodded. "She's a faerie, isn't she?" He nodded. "Take her to rest. And when she wakes, you must give her as much fresh juice as you can get her to drink. Then give her more. She'll die if you don't."

Burke nodded and turned with Piper in his arms. As he made his way to one of the suites that they used when there were family that needed attending to, his mind was as blank as it had ever been. Standing in front of the door, he stared at it as if...well, he wasn't sure. Then it opened and he stepped inside. Laying her on the bed, he watched her face and could hear the slow beating of her heart.

Searching the cupboards, he found all the blankets he could and put them over her. Piper's skin was cold...not just cool, but cold as ice. There was a thermostat in the room, and he turned it to as high as he could get it. He had no idea why he knew this, but she needed to be hot. Even as he emptied all the cupboards, he lifted the phone by the bed to his ear. Burke called to the nurse's station to get more blankets, as many as they could find. When Chris came in with Joey, he wasn't sure what to do. Then his grandma and grandda came in and both of them sat near Piper's bed.

"She's so weak." Chris nodded. "Can you do something for her? Make her better? Anything? She's my mate."

"I can't do anything for her, Burke. She knew what was going to happen as soon as she touched Gracie." He asked if she was going to die. "She might. Pip was weak before she touched her. And if she hadn't gotten the juice she had before this, she wouldn't have been able to help your mom. This has drained her nearly to the point of no return. Had I known this might happen, I would have insisted that she drink more earlier."

He sat down. His mate had saved his mom at the risk of killing herself. It occurred to him that might have been why she did it, but he didn't want to think that right now. Reaching up under the blankets, he took her cold hand into his.

"She wants to die." Neither of them said anything to him.

"I held her in my arms and I could feel how badly she wants to end her life. Had it not been for Franklin in the other room, I'm sure she would have done it by now."

"Franklin kept her from leaping to her death a few years ago. He held her for twenty minutes while he talked to her. Finally, he climbed over the railing of the building with her and told her that he'd go too. If he couldn't save one little girl from hurting herself, then he had nothing to live for either. He's been keeping an eye on her since." Burke figured she'd tried it before. He asked Chris if she knew why. "Yes. But that's something she needs to tell you, not me."

"I understand." Micah came into the room with Reggie and Grandma. "How's Mom? Is she going to be all right?"

"Yes. She went out back to shift and is resting now. I asked her to stay a cat for a little while, just to get herself better. I've never been so terrified in all my life as when that car came at us." His grandma sobbed as she continued. "She saved me. Gracie pushed me right out of the way, along with that little girl and her momma. If it hadn't been for her thinking fast...she saved us all."

Burke could see his mom doing that. No matter what, his mom would have dived in head first to save someone. He didn't even look away from Piper when he heard the door open and close again. He needed her to wake up and tell him what she'd meant by what she'd said about saving his mom because they were mates. And he was going to tell her that he loved her.

~~~

Micah tossed the book on the table. For all he knew it could have been telling him the meaning of life. The language there was nothing that he'd ever seen before, and he was pretty sure that most people wouldn't have known it either. It was faerie. He looked up when Reggie came into the room with him with

39

their daughters.

"That's perfect timing." He took one of them and marveled at how big they were getting. They smiled and cooed now, and he was loving every minute he could spend with them. As soon as Alexia smiled at him, Micah thought he could take on the world.

"I just talked to your mom. She would like to have dinner with all of us when Pip wakes up. She knows that Burke won't leave her, so she suggested that we wait." Micah saw his mom on the gurney every time he closed his eyes. He was pretty sure they all would for a very long time. "Also, the man that hit her, he swears that your mom jumped in front of him and is saying that he's going to sue her for damages to his car."

"Are you fucking kidding me? He came up on the sidewalk and hit her." Reggie nodded and then looked at Alexia. They were both trying to curb their cursing in front of the children. "I hope that Joey is on top of this."

"You have no idea. I guess he went to the man's house last night and ripped him a new butt. The police were called. It was a mess. Finally, the man confessed that he might have had a little too much to drink, but he's still saying that Gracie caused it all. The other family, the one with the little girl? They're suing him for all kinds of stuff. He's a fool if he thinks he can walk away from this with nothing more than a higher insurance deductible."

"I heard from the Mason attorney. Just so you know, I've talked to Chris and Joey about that too. And in the interest of being fair, they're not going to get in on this. Other than what they found out from Shane. For now, they've pulled him from school too. Shane was getting some pretty hard knocks from the boys' buddies." Reggie told him she'd like five minutes with those kids. "You and me both. The problem is, if we hurt them, we'll be up shit...up the creek without a boat, as Grandda says. But their attorney said that he has something that says that the plan had been Shane's all along and that he was the one with the drugs. The rest we've left untold for now. The school is aware of this, as are the girl's parents. Without some other proof, what do we have? It would be our word against his. Also, and this is a real kicker, the Masons are still going away for two weeks, leaving their sons with the house staff, and gave them permission to have a party anyway. I tell you, anyone tries this on one of my children, I'm not going to able to contain my cat."

"I'm looking into the female staff at the Mason building. If this is true, and I have no doubt that it is about Mason using the drug on his staff, then there has to be someone somewhere that'll talk. They've had a lot of women quitting without notice over the last five years, but I'm having a hard time finding them. It's like they left there and simply disappeared." He asked her if she thought they were dead. "I'm not sure yet. I hope not. That would really be just horrific. Oh, and there are some people trying to get us to talk to Burke. They want him to come back to work at the hospital. I told the one man I spoke to that he should simply fuck off."

Micah laughed. "I'm sure that he took that well. I heard from Burke about it yesterday. He said that he has no desire to go back and that he's ignoring their calls and emails." She asked him if he thought that was going to work out. "I have no idea, but Burke is the most relaxed I've seen him in a long time."

They talked about a few other things that needed to be taken care of. Mostly pack meetings and issues there. And when Alexia was sleeping, he gave her over to Reggie so she could put them both down in their beds to rest. He looked at his computer, trying his best to get up the energy to get to work. There was just too much on his mind. When his grandda came in his office and just sat down, Micah hoped to Christ it wasn't anything bad.

"That place I have down the street from the shelter, the one that we were thinking of putting in some apartments. What do you know about it?" He asked his grandda what he meant. "You remember that man that used to come in and cook for us once in a while? Elroy Baker?"

"The chef, that Elroy Baker? No, I don't remember him cooking for us. I would have remembered that." His grandda nodded. "What do you need to know about the buildings that might have to do with a five-star chef that has his own television program?"

"His wife died." That was sad news, and he told his grandda that. "I'll tell him you send your condolences. But he wants quiet now. I guess it was a long illness and he took care of her when she was ill, and now he just wants someplace to make a few meals that aren't gonna be graded every time he puts it in front of someone."

"He wants to put a small restaurant here? In our town?" Grandda said that was his plan. "I'm sure we can do better than one of the empty buildings in the downtown area. There is little parking down there, and most of them are storied places, not a single floor plan."

"He wants to live up on the upper floor, he told me. He has it in his head that he wants to do this low key. I'm not sure how he thinks that's gonna happen, but I told him I'd talk to you." Micah still wasn't sure what this man wanted. "Micah, he said that he just wants to cook, not be bothered by anyone."

"We'll do what we can for your friend, Grandda. I'm not sure what he'll want in the way of buildings, but I know that there are plenty to choose from there." He nodded. "What else? There has to be a reason why he's coming here. There are any number of small towns that he could hide out in."

"I'm not sure myself right now. I'm to have dinner with him tomorrow. He's human but knows what we are. And he really did cook for us when he was younger. I think your daddy thought him a little flaky, but he liked him." That was as good as an endorsement as he'd ever need for someone. "I was wondering if you can have that little wife of yours do some looking around. I just don't feel...it's not that I don't think this man is on the up and up, but there is something off about it. You know what I mean?"

"Yes." Grandda nodded. "Let me do some thinking on it too, okay? Maybe some of my sixth sense, as Dad used to call it, will kick in again. It's been a while since I've thought about it."

"You do that. Yes, sir, you do that." Grandda stood up and so did Micah. He had to find something to do or go insane. "Micah, this young woman that is Burke's mate. What do you think would drive a person to want to end their life?"

"I would say everything. I've been looking into it as well. Burke will have to be careful with her for a while, at least until he can convince her that she's going to be loved. I'm not even sure that will work. Some people who fight depression as much as she appears to have very little to no control over what they feel. And from what Chris said, she's pretty bad."

"Poor girl. That poor girl." Micah agreed. He also felt sorry for his brother. "And her being a faerie and all too. Nolan said that some of the drugs that help won't affect her a bit. I just hope they can work this out. We'll all have to work to keep her safe too."

He was still trying to understand depression. Micah was sure that it was more than likely the most misunderstood disease in the world. Once in line at the bank, he heard a man tell a woman he was standing by to just get over it. If she thought happy things, then she'd be happy. He also informed her that she was too depressing to be around. Micah had made it his business to learn as much as he could about depression, and the sad truth was, there was little out there about it.

As soon as he exited his office, he could smell it. The kitchen was in testing mode. He looked at Grandda and the both of them smiled. He was looking forward to tonight's dinner more than anything he'd had before.

"They said that we can't go in there until we're summoned." Micah felt like someone had taken his favorite candy bar from him. "Yeah, feel that way myself. This pre-Thanksgiving thing is just gonna kill me. Your grandma told me I was to take small portions, not try and see if I could finish each item. I tell you, there are times when I think she's trying to kill me."

"Or she could be trying to keep you healthy for your great-grandchildren." He nodded, but he still looked saddened by it. "I'll tell you what, if I find something I'm not really liking, I'll give you my part."

"Liar. You're just teasing an old man. And all I've done for you." Micah laughed. "Oh, before I forget. That man at the jeweler called and said to tell you that it's ready. You getting something special for my Reggie?"

"I did. And it might do you some good to get something nice for Grandma. She might cut you some slack." He nodded and said he'd give it some thought.

Micah wasn't sure why he bothered telling Grandda that. He was the most romantic man he knew. Grandda would come in with a dozen roses for Grandma when Micah was younger. Even now he would just hand her a box of something and act like it was no big deal to have gotten it. The other day he'd given a list and some pictures to the pawn shop, asking them to keep an eye on something for him. Grandma collected tea cups, and it was Grandda's mission in life, it seemed, to get her every one that came into town.

Reggie didn't collect things, but he might have found something that she'd like. An ornament that had been found in a box in the attic. Mom had told him she'd never seen it before, but it might have been left by some other family member before them. Whoever it was, they had excellent taste.

The clear globe had been handmade, of that he was sure. What he'd not known and was surprised by, was that it was over a hundred years old, and that the workmanship in it, the town scene, had been hand painted by someone, then the glass blown up around it. The panthers had been placed around the village in the most beautiful settings. One was lying at the bottom of the Christmas tree. Another was in a small open field. Two were obviously at play on the town square. Micah had fallen in love with it, and had taken it in to be cleaned up a week ago.

He hoped she loved it as much as he did. If not, well, he'd just keep it for himself. Smiling, he followed his nose and his grandda into the kitchen. It was about lunch time anyway. Then he was going to find someone to help him with that book that Myra had given him this morning.

Chapter 4

Pip woke up shaking. She was freezing to death and felt like she was being buried alive at the same time. When a face, blurry and dark, moved in front of her, she screamed and tried to get away. When he spoke, she calmed just a little, but was still not sure what was going on.

"I have some juice for you. Can you sit up for me?" She did and remembered the man, but she was too cold and weak to put things together right now. "I'm Burke. I was told you might not remember a lot at first. That the power you used sort of takes from all of you. Here, baby, take as much as you can stand right now."

"Your mom." He nodded. "She's well then? She survived the accident. I helped her. With your help, correct?"

"Yes. I had to ask about that. I had no idea when you said that because of us being mates that we could heal her." She drank the juice down and the glass refilled. "Myra did that for you. She said that as long as it refilled for you that you needed to keep emptying it. I had about forty or so glasses before it finally stopped."

"I have to go to the bathroom." Burke nodded and took the still full glass and set it on the dresser next to her. "I can manage on my own. I'm fine now."

"No, you're not. And even if you could manage on your own, I can't. I can't...seeing you like you've been for the last twenty-four hours scared the fuck out of me." She let him help her up...she was a good deal weaker than she'd ever been before. "Mom and my sisters sent you over some clothes. Myra, she said that you'd be cold for a few hours after you woke up. She never said why, but I think I have it figured out. Energy; you have to replace it, and shaking does that."

"Yes." He helped her into the bathroom, and that was when she realized that she wasn't in a hospital. "Where am I? And how on earth did I get here?"

"Yeah, about that. I brought you here last night. And this? It's our home. I didn't have anything to do with it, but apparently leaving you at the shelter was going to cause problems. I guess there wasn't any way for the magic to keep all the people out who might have harmed you. Myra said that no one would enter if she had her way, and decided that you'd be better off in our home." Pip asked him how that had worked and him not having anything to do with his house. "I was looking for one. The last several weeks, as a matter of fact. When I told her that, she said it wouldn't do. That we had one."

"I don't really see, but I guess it's your home." Before he could say anything, she closed the door in his face. She heard him laughing, and for some reason that made her smile. But that disappeared as soon as she looked in the mirror. "Oh my."

She was as pale as the counter under her hands. She knew that she had used a lot of her magic to heal Mrs. Bentley, but with her having a mate—because there was little doubt now that he was her mate—her magic along with her energy had been depleted to the point where it was evident on her body. Pip let her wings go to see how badly they were harmed.

"You okay?" She didn't answer him; she wasn't sure what her answer would have been had she tried. Her wings were...were beautiful. Everything about them was beautiful and colorful. Like someone had captured a rainbow and had splashed it at her wings. "Can you please let me in? I can feel something going on. It's like I know that you're using magic and that I need to be near you. Please?"

Not sure why she felt he needed to be with her either, she opened the door. He stared at her and then had her turn. She did so, holding onto anything that was close enough so she'd not fall.

"They didn't look like that before, did they? I mean, I only saw them for a little bit, but I'm pretty sure that they're different." She nodded her head. "And they're...they were beautiful before, but now they're amazing. Can I touch them?"

"Just be careful with them. I don't know what you'll do if— Fuck."

His touch brought her to peak. It was too much and not enough. When he put his hands on both of her wings, Pip held onto him as he took her mouth. It was erotic and sexy, the way he made her feel with just a touch.

"I need you." She nodded, stripping off his clothing as he tore at hers. "Christ, I'm so close to coming that I feel like if you touched me, I'd explode."

"Inside of me. Please. I need to feel you inside of me." He nodded, and when he was naked, he dropped to his knees in front of her. Before she could tell him that wasn't going to be enough, that she needed his cock, he took her pussy into his mouth and bit down on her clit.

She wasn't prepared for the climax. Pip knew she'd been close, the several he'd given her with his fingers on her wings had given her a lot. But his mouth on her, his tongue fucking her, took her so hard, so beautifully, that it was all she could do to hang onto consciousness. And yet he never stopped no matter how much she begged him to.

Come for me, Burke told her in her head. *I need to drink as much of you as I can before I fill you with my cock. My cat wants to taste you as well. He needs his mate.*

"Yes, please. I need it as well."

The man, the beautiful man, was gone, and in his place was the most gorgeous panther she'd ever seen. And as soon as he buried his mouth over her, she screamed again and again until she was weak from her releases. Her body burned with need as much as it did from how much he was giving her. Even as she begged him to stop, pleaded that she could take no more, Burke was there, lifting her up and sliding her down over his cock.

He was thick, hard, and filled her to the brim. Burke held her to him, never moving as her body adjusted to his. And when he did take her, picking her up and holding her to his body, she cried out as a climax nearly took her under.

He fucked her against the wall, with his hands holding her. He moved to the bed again, not stopping his mouth from branding her as it moved along her skin, tasting and biting her. When she was wrapped around him, her legs securely behind him, Burke laid down with her body wrapped around his, filled with him. He took her nipple in his mouth and bit down hard on it, causing her to cry out again and again as he pleased her.

And when he fucked her, his cock slamming forward so fully, she held him to her, knowing that he was indeed her mate.

The climax was painfully beautiful. His cock filled her over and over as he moved his way up to her throat with his mouth again, and the pounding pulse she knew that was there. Pip stopped him this time with a jerk to his hair.

"You bite me and we're one." He nodded. "If I bite you then we're the same. Do you understand what that means? My blood will be yours."

"Yes. I understand. We'll be mated and bonded as a pair." Pip wasn't sure that he really understood her, but before she could try to explain more, he nipped at her throat. "Come for me, Piper. I want to taste you while you come."

She came. Not just with her body, but her mind, too, came apart. It was overwhelming the way that she seemed to need more, as it was too much. When she came again, too many times to even count now, Pip held him to her as his teeth grazed her throat. And the moment he bit down, she sank her fangs down into his shoulder at the same time.

Her magic transferred to him the moment he sucked at the wound he'd made. It wasn't as if it drained her, but balanced her with him. They were the same, he as her, and she as him. It was the way of her kind. As he came, crying out around her flesh, she closed her eyes and let the magic fill them both.

His thoughts became hers. All his memories were now hers as well. And while she knew that he could read her mind before, this would be different. He'd know her, completely and fully, as well as he did himself. Memories, hers and his, would be shared. Magic as well. Touching his back, reaching for the scapula at his shoulder, she could feel them forming; his wings would be as beautiful as hers had become. And when he dropped onto her, Pip knew a sadness that she'd never felt before. He was as she was. The sadness took her breath away and the tears began to fall.

"Don't cry." She nodded at his words, and when his fingers touched her cheeks she held them there. "It's fine, Piper. I should have known that we'd share your magic. It's fine."

"It's not fine, don't you see? You are faerie, just as I am." He nodded. "No, you don't understand. You're like me. A faerie. A freak of nature. People will scorn you, hunt you down and try to kill you."

"They might, but I'm also a panther. I can feel him there. He's confused as much as I am about what is happening to us, but we're happy that you're ours." She sat up when he rolled to his back. "Piper, I swear to you, it's going to be fine."

"Stop saying that. Do you know what your family is going to say? What they'll do?" He said that they'd love her as much as he did already. "No. No one loves me, Burke. I'm not human. I'm nothing like you are."

"You are everything to me." He got up then and stopped moving when he was dressed suddenly. "Did you do that?"

"No, you did. You were thinking about having an argument naked." He nodded and grinned. "This is not funny."

"You dress for me. I want to see you in something pretty and warm. Then you can drink some more juice." She just stared at him. "You need to wear green to go with your eyes. I mean, a sexy red dress would be awesome too, but for now, something that I feel I can let you leave this room in without stripping you down again. Here, drink this."

She did as he said and watched the glass fill again. At the rate it was filling, she'd be buzzing soon. Pip drank three more glasses before it filled only half full this time. Burke was pacing. She was afraid to look at his thoughts, knowing that he was just realizing what they'd done.

"You have fangs, right?" She nodded. "Will I as well? I'm guessing so. And wings. I know those are there. I'm not ready to spread them yet. I'm working up to it. I'm worried that they'll be ugly compared to yours."

"Are you listening to what you're saying? You have wings, Burke. And fangs. You're a fucking panther with wings." He looked at her and she could see what he was thinking. "No, your panther will not be able to fly. Christ, you're acting like this is no big deal."

He pulled her to him and kissed her. "It's not a big deal. I have a sister-in-law that is the grand witch of all witches. Pretty awesome stuff that. Another one can feel the pain of horses. She talks to them, actually, and they talk back to her. Reggie, she's Micah's wife, has this pretty amazing power too. She's a mom. To the prettiest little twin girls you've ever seen. I have a brother-in-law, Boyd, that they just found out can paint. He's had some tragic brain injuries, but he can use his mouth to hold a brush and can paint these beautiful pictures that make you want to sob. My brothers and mom are panthers, as you know, but they're immortal. All of us are. So you and I being faeries is small stuff in comparison."

When she started to tell him again that he was not the same any more, he put his hand over her mouth. She looked into his eyes and could see that he really was in love with her. He smiled as he continued to talk to her.

"We have a home, something that I've only thought about several million times a day since I quit working so hard. And not only do we have it, but it's magical as well. Filled with the things that we both wanted in a home. You have excellent taste by the way. I've even made arrangements to have Franklin taken to a facility that is very close to us until he's improved enough to come and live with us. He'll need some care, but he'll be close to you. Where you both need him to be." She pulled his hand away. "I'm a simple doctor, Piper. A man who, up until a few months ago, thought that I was a failure at everything I'd done so far. I was in a job that I hated, working with people that I disliked even more. And my family seemed to be moving toward goals in their life that I didn't think I'd ever have. And now here you are."

"Yes, here I am." He kissed her again. "What happens if—?" He cut her off with his mouth again. Burke was pretty good at it too, and when he lifted his head, she huffed at him. "Are you going to do that every time I want to say something that you don't like?"

"Yes. I think I will." He kissed her again. "Okay, no more fooling around. My mom has invited us over for pre-Thanksgiving tasting. She's never done this before, so it's a big deal to her."

"What is that?" He explained. "So she wants to try some different dishes out and you guys are the taste testers? Does she cook all that well?"

"No, not well at all, but that's not the point. Meggie, she's the cook, she's doing it all. My mom has gone all over the Internet looking for different things to eat, and Meggie is making them. She makes a great apple pie too." Pip sat down when he gave her a little shove. "Shoes. You need to put on shoes."

Reaching into his mind, she saw that he had a shoe thing. Not a fetish, but he loved sexy shoes on women. Finding a pair that he'd like the most, she put them on her feet. His reaction was priceless.

"We're going to be late." He was naked in seconds and told her to strip as well. "But leave the shoes on. I love them."

~~~

Gracie watched the couple. She knew there was something different about them both, other than that they were bonded and mated, but she couldn't put her finger on it. She had to smile when Pip smacked Burke every time he touched her. As a cat, he was prone to love the feel of his mate near him, but apparently Pip wasn't used to it yet. She would be. When Meggie came to tell them that dinner was ready, they moved to the door, but she pulled Pip aside for a moment.

"You saved my life." Pip shook her head. "You did and we both know it. I knew as soon as that glass entered me that there wasn't going to be any saving me. I was as good as dead. Even as close as I was to the shelter."

"Burke helped." She knew that as well. "He and I are mates. I don't think he understands what he got from me in this relationship. He's like I am."

It took Gracie several moments to figure out what she'd meant. But then Pip had moved on and she was standing alone in the hall. Burke was a faerie as well. Smiling, she wondered what the girl would say if she told her that she didn't care if she was a lizard, so long as she and Burke were happy.

Everyone was filling plates by the time she entered the dining room. There were side dishes, as well as a few glazes on two different hams that they'd baked. There were more desserts than she had counted on, but Thanksgiving had taken on a new meaning since Reggie had joined their family. And since last year, she felt herself getting more and more excited for the holidays all the time. She was even working on a plan for Memorial Day, a holiday that had been her husband's favorite. Gracie made her way to Katie when she had a full plate of some of the sides.

"I don't think I care for the potatoes. What is in them?" She told her that it looked like capers. "No, I don't care for those.

But this pasta thing, my goodness this is good. And those rolls. Did Reggie make those?"

"She gave me the recipe. Our cook has been using a lot of the older versions of recipes that she's unearthed. She and Reggie think that it's more rib sticking for the people that they feed." Katie agreed. "What else have you tried?"

"None of the desserts yet. And so you know, I'm going to be keeping an eye on Howie too. I don't really care if he eats one of each piece. He's just not going to hog the entire pies like he normally does." She laughed with her. "Now, we've done the small talk thing. Tell me what's bothering you. Is it the blanket you're knitting? I told you that you need to tighten your stitches."

"I have, it's coming along beautifully. And I think I might even have it finished before Chris has her baby. I was going to talk to you about Burke and Pip." Katie told her they were beautiful together. "I agree. But she told me that he's like she is. I'm thinking she meant faerie."

"Does that bother you?" She said that it didn't, but she thought it might be bothering Pip. "Why on earth would that...? Oh, I see. She thinks that we might be upset about it. Yes, I can see that. The poor girl has a very low opinion of herself. I'm thinking it has to do with her being so down and hurting all the time. I cannot imagine what it would be like to be like that all the time. The poor thing. She will need us to keep her in our thoughts all the time, don't you think?"

"I do. I've been talking to a friend of mine. His wife suffered so terribly with depression. So much so that she took her own life rather than hurt with it. He said the best thing not to do is to tell her that she needs to get over it. There is no getting over it for a person who suffers from this. And he said that sometimes we'll have to take her out of her comfort zone and take a walk, go to the movies or dinner with her. We're not to let her just hide away. That'll be the worst." Katie told her that it would be up to them to get her out when Burke was working. "She needs to find a job, too, Burke was telling me. He seems to think that finding something that she can work at and think of besides being depressed would get her mind off how she was feeling. Not completely, but enough that she's not to hurt by this."

"Oh, what a wonderful idea. Do you suppose that she'll be any good at organizing things?" Gracie said she had no idea. "I need help with the Christmas auction."

"Katie, that might be too much for anyone, much less a person that we hardly know." Katie told her she'd be perfect at it. "I don't know. I was thinking something smaller, like a garden or working at the shelter."

"No, no, she needs something to keep her hands and mind busy. This will be perfect, I know it." Gracie wasn't so sure but let Katie run with it. She looked around, and that was when she saw young Shane sitting alone. Before she could get up and go to him, Pip sat down next to him.

Gracie worried for the boy. She'd gotten him into this private school, and she was finding out that it was no better or safer than any of the rest of the ones around. Just bullies with more money to burn, that was all. She smiled when Pip sat down with Shane and wondered what they were talking about.

"They are conspiring." She looked over at Howie when he sat where Katie had been. Gracie hadn't even realized she'd left her. "Shane is a good boy. You don't have to worry much about him."

"I worry about my boys and they're grown men. One little boy is nothing compared to how much I worry for them." Howie laughed, and she noticed that he had about a quarter of the lemon tart pie that had been part of the desserts. "You're going to get into trouble if you keep eating like that. What if Katie sees you?"

"It's for you." She eyed him shrewdly. "Oh all right, it wasn't for you, but if you want it, I'll share. I like this one most of all. The way you candied up them lemons on the top."

"Meggie didn't want to throw them out, so we looked up a way to use them. I have a bunch left over in the freezer that I thought we could use in homemade ice cream some time." He nodded while he shoved another bite full into his mouth. "Burke is a faerie like Pip is."

She pounded him hard on the back when he started coughing. Every time he looked at her with watery eyes, she had to laugh more. Gracie hadn't planned on making him choke, but it had been fun once she'd done it. He wasn't going to keel over, but he did milk it a little longer than was necessary, she thought.

"You're just mean. You know that girly? Just plain mean." She smiled at him. "That ain't no way to tell a man something. When his mouth was filled up."

"If I waited until your mouth was empty, Howie, I'd never be able to tell you anything." He glared, then laughed. "You are a man that loves his food. But back to Burke, I think Pip is upset about it."

"Why for?" He ate another bite of food, but it was much smaller this time. And when he had finished and swallowed, he continued. "Ain't nothing to get your panties all in a bunch over if you're thinking it's a bad thing. Is it?"

"No, and I said she was upset, not me. I think it's wonderful. I wonder what sort of things they can do together." She glanced over at Pip and Shane again. "She's so lovely, don't you think, Howie? Not like the others aren't, but there is something so calming and serene about her that I find myself wanting to be near her."

"She's a mite touchy about things, but I think we can bring her around. I feel badly for her though. Carrying around that horrible burden. But if anyone can keep her safe, it's Burke. He's a good man for her." Gracie agreed. "You think him being a faerie and all that his cat will fly? I think I'd pay real money to see that, I surely would."

"Howie, what am I going to do with you?" She looked at her son and smiled. The way he kept looking as his mate, she wondered if there would be another announcement soon. She loved being a grandmother almost as much as she did being a mom. And the girls were the best there were too…all her daughters-in-law were.

Gracie thought of her late husband and knew that he'd be in the thick of things right now. Egging on his father, teasing the boys. And loving those grandchildren as much as she did. Gracie missed him so much, but with the family around, she felt she could deal with the pain a good deal better than alone.

Chapter 5

"So this kid at school was going to use a date drug on a girl you know." Shane nodded and Pip smiled. "That was really brave of you to do that for her. Most people I know wouldn't have bothered with it at all. If she were my daughter, I'd be glad that you did it. Is anyone giving you any shit about it?"

"No, they're all being really nice about it, telling me how wonderful it is that I helped her. She's really nice. But older than me." Shane looked around before continuing. "Martha, her name is Martha. They tease her about that too, like a name is something someone gets to pick out."

"I did." He looked up at her. "You know that I'm not human, right? I wasn't born like the rest of you were either. Especially not you. I was hatched. But I was walking along the waterway and I saw this big tanker in the water. It had Cordale on it. And I liked the way that water sounded when it dripped into the bay. A pip-pip sound."

"No way. You can't have.... Really? You were hatched?" She nodded. "Right out of an egg and everything? You were hatched out of an egg like a chicken?"

"No, it was a bud. A flower." He asked her if she was pulling his leg. "Not at all. I know that I'm bigger than a flower, but I wasn't always this size. Anyway, when the fields where I was created were just coming into bloom, the queen of all the faeries came around and touched the buds of the newly formed flowers. Some of the older plants, like the perennials, they had done this before, but not the one that I came from. She was a tulip, a pink one."

"No kidding?" She could tell that he didn't really believe her. But she wasn't lying to him. "And when you were ready to come out, what happened to you then? You would have been so tiny that you'd have gotten lost in the grass."

"No. Some do, but not me. There are other faeries that come to collect us and take us to the tip top of the trees to get lots of sunlight. Some of them are forgotten in the flowers. There are a great many of us born, and those that are dropped into the earth when the flower is ready to open, they become brownies." He eyed her suspiciously. "I'm not kidding, Shane. That is the way true faeries are born. You can ask Myra when she comes again. She'll know."

"She's here now. Her and Aunt Chris are talking about witch stuff." Pip watched Shane as he stood up. He was waiting for her to tell him never mind, but she wouldn't. As he made his way to Myra, he was sure that he was going to be the butt of a great joke. She knew the moment he'd been told she was telling him the truth. When he came back and sat down, she could see on his face that he wasn't sure if he believed her, but he would give her the benefit of the doubt. "She said that you sharing this with me makes us special."

"Yes. Not many people know how a true faerie is made or born." He nodded. "Thank you for believing in me. By the way, did you know that you have a dragon that watches over you? He's a blue dragon. The one on your closet door."

"Nah, he's just a...." He looked at her with his eyes wide. "Myra said that you can't lie to me. Is that right?"

"True. I can't lie to anyone. I can give half-truths, like leave some parts out, but for the most part, everything I say has to be the truth." He nodded. "There is a dragon. And he protects you. Did you know that?"

"But he's only a painting on my closet. Of course, I talk to him. Every night, I tell him about my day and things like that. So you say that he's there? A real dragon that watches over me? How does he come to me?" She lifted his arm up and waved her hand over the smoothness of his pre-adult skin. The dragon appeared there, his body fully formed, and when he moved, Shane jerked his hand from her. After a few minutes, he gave it back to her. "Can I only see him when you do that?"

"When you turn thirteen, he'll come to you. Like a sigil that your uncle and I both have now." She pulled her own sleeve up and showed it to him, careful of the scars at her wrist that she'd put there one night in despair. "Your Aunt Chris will have a mark, as well as your Uncle Joey. They're mates and they share it. Mine is my own and Burke has one that is similar, but it's male. See? Mine is a female. You will have your dragon with you for the rest of your days and share him with your own mate, or in your case, someone that you fall in love with. Did you name your dragon?"

He nodded. "I have to just call him? When I need him? That seems...well, too easy. What if I just say his name and he comes running?"

"Don't tell anyone his name, not even your parents. Not because they'll use him, because they can't. But it's magical. Just between the two of you." Shane asked her how that worked. "You and he will figure that out. Within the confines of your magic, in this case your room, for now. And you have to remember, Shane. When you call him to you because you really need him, you need to know that when he comes, he will destroy whatever is there. Not your family, but any other creature there, including any kind of creatures that are helping you as well. Do you understand? Every creature. That might be all right to save your life. But if you call him to show off, they're all dead."

Pip watched his face. He would understand it, she knew this. The boy was smart and he had a great many people around him that had shown him what magic was all about. When he looked back at her, she could see fear, yet understanding, on his face.

"Thank you, Aunt Pip. I might have hurt someone had you not told me." She explained that the dragon would have told him that and more. "But I know now, and that is going to help me not freak out when he does show up. I think I might have too. A big dragon...he will be big, right?"

"Very." He grinned at her. "You're a cute kid. You know that, right? There are going to be women fighting over you when you're older, I think."

"Nah, women are for the others. I just want to grow up and be like my uncles. Smart enough to be making money, yet not stupid enough to spend it on dumb stuff like fast cars and stuff." Pip told him that it didn't always work out that way. "I know. But I can hope. Besides, girls are just weird. I see them at school and they act like they're all that. When I know that most of them don't have a clue."

"I don't." He looked at her. "This entire family terrifies me. I don't like...I have some days when I just don't see the point of getting up and getting going. It's hard on me."

"You should go fishing with Great-Grandda. He talks a lot, but he gets around to telling you the thing to do. Most of the time when we go it's never quiet, but he doesn't get on your nerves with it." He looked over at the elderly man and so did she. "He's the best. And Great-Grandma too. All of them are, I think. They sure do love you if you let them. Are you going to let them, Aunt Pip?"

"I'm working my way up to it." He nodded and stood up. "You remember what I told you. And there is something else you should know. That if you need me, for any reason, I can get there faster than anyone else. And take you away to safety, too."

"Because you can fly." She nodded at him. "I'll remember that. I promise that when my dragon and I talk, I'll tell him what a wonderful person you are too. I read that faeries and dragons are friends."

"We help each other." Shane nodded and moved away. Almost as soon as she'd decided that she wanted some peace, Tony sat beside her. This was one Bentley that had been hard to understand. She put out her hand and he stared at it before speaking.

"I'm not sure I want you to know all about me." She said nothing. In fact, she didn't need to touch him to know what hurt him. "There are people here that would pay you well to find out what ails me, as Grandda says."

"You aren't sick." He shook his head. "You should talk to them. I've noticed that they're overbearing and pushy, but they love you very much. They're worried for you."

"And you." She said nothing but left her hand out. "You

don't need that, do you? My touch to know what's in my head. I have a feeling that no matter how hard I block you, you can and will get in. Or have you already?"

"I don't trust well. And I want to know the beings that I will have to spend time with. You are...you're an enigma to me, if you want to know the truth." He asked her why. "Because, contrary to everyone's belief, you aren't the quiet type, nor are you a partier. You're more of a go-to man, aren't you? Women, men, even children know that if they have a problem or a question, you'll give it to them straight up."

He said nothing for several moments. "I've been hurt. Badly. My heart has been...I don't think that it's mendable. I'm not even sure that I want it to be. I lost my mate to someone. He killed her before I could help her out of the situation." Pip said nothing to him but let him continue. "I should have done something, anything other than to just sit back and let him kill her. I might have been happy had I done something."

"I doubt that you did nothing. But as for happiness or whatever it is you think you've lost, it's there, just waiting for someone. Or is it that you've given up? You had your one shot at happiness and you aren't going to go out and find it again?" He said they only got one chance. "I don't think that the fates are that cruel. It's been my experience that if something fails for them, they simply move things around until they're the way that they want them."

"You mean you and Franklin." She nodded. They knew the story as well as she did, she supposed. "He told me the other day when I went to check on someone else that you and he were destined to be friends. He said that you had it in your head that you were going to die that day, and that there wasn't much he could to other than to join you. He told me that he was really glad that you'd come back to him. He didn't want to make a mess on the sidewalk." He'd told her the same thing back then; he'd make a mess while he knew she'd be beautiful.

"He has grandchildren. They don't have anything to do with him, but they're all he talks about." Tony nodded, and she knew that he'd seen the pictures as well as heard about them. "The youngest one in those photos is nearly your age now. It's been that long since he's had any contact with them. He'd been in the service for most of his life, and they sort of slipped away from him. His daughter, she died some time back, and her kids sort of forgot about him. Probably a good thing too."

"I looked into his life. Like you, I want to know the beings that I spend time with." Pip figured that at some point, they had all looked into each of their lives to see what they were up against. "His daughter is dead, as you said, but the kids are living it up in a lovely home. There is a boy and girl, as you know, but they are telling people that they have no family at all. And you're right, the grandchildren that he loves so much are shits and would cross the street to avoid anyone like him."

"He knows that too." Tony said he figured as much. "You never answered me. What are you going to do about life, Anthony? Just let it pass you by?"

"Are you going to try and kill yourself again?" She looked at him and gave him the most honest answer she could. "I see. Well, I guess saying you don't know is better than a flat out yes. In answer to your question. I'm not sure either. I just... what would be the point?"

"The point is all around you." He looked around when she did. "You're unhappy. So are they. You get on with your life, even if it's only to please them, then I'm betting that they don't walk around on egg shells when you're around. Nor will they try and hide things from you because they don't want to hurt you any more than you already are."

"I know that they do that. And no matter how much I try to tell them that I'm okay, which I guess they know that I'm not, they still do it. I'm not depressed, not like you, but I do feel that there are times when I can't think what the point is. But I'll think on it." He sat there for several more moments before he turned to her. "I have a job for you should you want it. I think you'd be really good at it. I need someone to come in and organize things for me. I don't have anyone working with me other than a high school kid that is more trouble than he's worth."

"I don't like people." He said neither did he much, but he was a small animal vet. "And you want me to come in and help you with the cats and dogs of the world."

"There is an occasional bunny too, but I do. As I said, I think you'd be really good at it." She told him how she was going to help Rylee first on a project. "Good. That'll give me time to get things at least a little cleaned up. I've let the filing and business part of things go for a while."

He put out his hand. When she took it in hers, she felt the connection. "You won't like me working for you. I'm going to tell you that now."

"That's all right. You're not going to like working for me. But I think we'll suit." When he walked away, she stood up and made her way to the kitchen. She needed to be outdoors for a few moments.

~~~

Burke wasn't sure if he should follow her or not. Piper had seemed upset when she left a few minutes ago, and he knew that his family could be a bit overwhelming. Excusing himself, he made his way to the deck at the back of the house and figured if she wasn't there, then he'd just wait for a little while longer before finding her. She was sitting on the steps that led into the yard.

"What am I supposed to do with you?" He asked her what she meant by that. "Just that. I've been pretty much on my own for as long as I can remember. I have no family really, unless you count others like me. Which, just so you know, I don't hang out with. I don't have any use for things that most women do. I like it quiet and peaceful. I'm not very good around crowds of people either. And here you are with five brothers, grandparents, a mom, and sisters-in-law, even nieces and nephews. You're all loud and pushy, and think that you know best when it comes to those around you."

He sat beside her, giving himself time to think of an answer. Burke had a feeling that this was as important to them and their relationship as loving her would be. He took her hand in his and was glad that she didn't pull away.

"I like it quiet as well. Not all the time…the thought of just going home right now and sitting on the couch with you sounds great. I don't think I saw a television in the house, but it matters little. I never watched one anyway. I take it you meant girly things?" She nodded. "I don't mind that either. To be honest with you, I'm not into clutter either. And while I wouldn't care one fig if you had fifty bottles of makeup and perfume on the counters all spread out, I love the fact that you're as natural as the outdoors and smell like my own little flower."

"That was sappy." He grinned at her. "I can't be like them all the time. Happy and friendly. I'm depressed. I need to be alone at times to think. I'm afraid that if I just be me, they'll take it out on you. And while I am taking a few meds now, thanks to you, sometimes they're just not strong enough for me. The things that would work for a human don't always work for me because I'm not. I don't want you hurt."

Burke picked her up and sat her on his lap. Holding her

made him feel better, and he held her thinking of their future together as a couple. It would be hard. He wasn't stupid enough to think that just because he had her in his life that she was suddenly going to be happy all the time. She hurt, then he did as well.

"I don't know how to help you when you need it. You'll have to tell me. Even if it's for me to go away and leave you alone. I'll never be far, but I'll do what it takes for you to get what you need." She sighed heavily. "But I would ask that you talk to me when you're feeling suicidal. I know that if you have someone to talk to it helps, and you can always talk to me, love."

"I know that, but there are times when I just don't know what I'm sad about. There is no trigger for it. I could be standing there, talking to someone and having a very enjoyable time. Then bam, it hits me and I want to drop to my knees, the pain is so tremendous. I have no control over it either. It washes over me in waves sometimes, and it's hard to recover from it before the next wave hits me." She snuggled up under his chin. "I've pushed people away all my life. I didn't want to have to explain to them why I was down. Hear from them that I just need to get over it. Shake it off. I can't do that. I'm not able to do that."

"I'll be here for you. And as much as I love you, my family does as well. And they'll be there for you as well." She told him that was the problem. "You mean because they'll hound you to death to be with them? Because they can't take no for an answer? Yes, I'm well aware of how they are. But they love you. And if you tell them to fuck off, they'll leave you alone. However, I would caution you about saying that to my mom. She can be a little touchy about being told that."

She looked at him. "You didn't tell your mom to fuck off,

did you?" He nodded. "Oh my God, Burke, what did she do to you? I'm sure that it wasn't nice."

"It wasn't. For four days I had to endure sitting with her on the couch and watching her favorite movies. While that wasn't so bad, I had to also write her an essay on the meaning of the term, as well as when it had originated in the human language. Ten thousand words. You try writing out an essay about two words that at the tender age of twelve had very little meaning other than shock value."

"I bet." She stood up and stretched. "You want to fly with me? I need to get up and around or hurt."

"You mean really fly?" She looked at him and asked him what else she'd mean. "I don't have a clue. But...well, I knew that I have wings but.... You really think I can fly?"

"You can if you want. I'm going to take off. If you want to wait here, that's fine." He stood up, as excited as he'd ever been before. "So? This is a yes? You want to fly with me?"

"Yes, very much so. But don't leave me behind if I falter." She assured him that he'd do well. "Yeah, well, I'm not as confident as you are."

Her laughter made his heart feel really good. And when she stretched out her wings and told him to do the same, he was almost afraid to. When the door to the deck opened behind him, he was almost afraid to turn. Burke looked at his family and groaned. Of course they would see him at what he was sure would be his worst.

"Go away." Trent sat down on one of the numerous chairs and waved at him. "Bastard. Why don't you all go away and leave me to fail in this on my own?"

"Go on boy, do it. I don't rightly know what it is you're about to do, but I'm sure you're gonna be great at it." He told his grandda that he was going to fly. "Fly? Well, I guess it was bound to happen sooner or later. Better to let us see you right up front so we don't go freaking out when we see you in the sky."

Piper took his chin in her hand and turned him to look at her. "Concentrate. If you do this right, we can be home and naked in bed before they figure out we're gone."

He heard Trent laugh again and decided that he was going to piss on him while he was in the sky one day. When Piper winked at him, he knew she had heard his thoughts. He thought about his cat and how he brought him forth, and did the same for his wings. When he heard the others on the deck whooping for him, he felt like he was on the right track.

"Now, this is the tricky part." He asked her what that was supposed to mean. "Well, you have to figure out how to get them going. Think of a bird, and then when they move, you have to look where you want to go. Just until you get upward."

"I'm not sure what you mean." She stepped back, and he watched her wings flutter. Then she looked upward and she soared to the sky. Again his family cheered from behind him. He wondered if they'd laugh just as hard if he fell to the earth and died. Thinking of getting his wings to work, he didn't turn to his family for fear of disappointing them. Instead he looked upward and felt himself move to the clouds.

"Holy shit, I did it." Piper laughed. It sounded so wonderful he wanted her to do it again. When he started to fall, she told him to watch what he was doing. "I guess I have to think about them all the time or I lose it. Right? I can do this."

"Not all the time, but you have to think about them enough to keep them moving for you. We can float, like a bird does on a current, but not too much. We're heavier and we aren't as aerodynamic as they are." She did just that for several minutes. "I'd not do this just yet if I were you. Just fly until you feel like you got the hang of that for now."

They played for over an hour. Every time he felt like he was getting the hang of it, he'd mess up and have to think about what he was doing again. It was exhilarating and scary at the same time. And when they landed in their yard, Burke pulled Piper into his arms and kissed her.

"Thank you." She asked him for what. "For making me into something that I love. For giving me wings. But most of all, thank you so much for simply being you. Christ, I love you so much."

She pulled away and he let her. She was dealing with it, he knew. And while he could have been hurt by it, he knew that whatever she was feeling was ten times more. Burke was going to be there for her, as much as she'd let him. And when she turned to him, he smiled at her and she smiled back.

"I'd like a greenhouse." He nodded without even thinking about anything but getting her what she wanted. "I know the house has some magical powers, so I'm thinking that it'll already be there. But I want to grow flowers that the other faeries can use."

"I'm not sure how that works, but whatever you want. Will a greenhouse be enough to get it started?" She nodded, then shook her head. "I want you happy, Piper. Tell me what you need."

"I need to contact Myra and Chris about it. While the faerie queen isn't in their realm of magic, I am now. I have to get permission from them to do this." He nodded, knowing there was more. "You'll have to be with me when we go to see her."

"I can do that. Anytime." She nodded but still didn't move. "Is this going to be bad? Or are you just nervous about seeing her?"

"I'd like to take young Shane with me." Again, he nodded,

but told her that his parents would have to know. "Yes, of course. He has a dragon. Did you know that? The queen might be able to tell him things that I don't know. And the book that your brother has? The one Myra gave him? He can read it now. Not that it's been translated, but I knew that he wanted to read it so I let him."

"He'll be happy about that. Micah loves to understand things completely." She nodded and looked at the house. "You're happy here, aren't you, Piper?"

"I am." She turned to him then. "The house is magical. I know that you're aware of that. But did you know that you can see it? All of it. And that if I can do this for the faeries, they'll be as much a part of this house as we are."

He looked at the house now and saw the blue lines of markings along every part of it. The roof was full of them, the walls as well. The windows, all of them top and bottom, were solid with the magic that kept them safe. Burke realized what she'd said about the faeries.

"You mean they'll live with us." She nodded. "Will they...I don't know. Will they be troublesome?"

"Oh yes, they'll be troublesome for sure." She grinned at him. "But they'll be wonderful to have here. I think you might like it a great deal."

He wasn't so sure. They'd just talked about being at peace here. He wondered what sort of trouble a few faeries were going to be. As they made their way into the house, he figured that he'd put up with just about anything to see her smile like she was right now. Even a real faerie garden in his yard.

Chapter 6

The grass under them was warm. Warmer than he'd thought it would be at eleven-thirty at night. They were to meet with the queen at midnight, the bewitching hour, he'd been told. Micah hadn't wanted to leave the house and his little girls, but now that he was here, he was very excited. He was about to meet a real faerie queen. He looked over at Reggie when she said his name.

"You promised to be good. And not to worry about the kids. Your mom is watching them, and your grandda is helping. Okay, maybe worry a little." He grinned and nodded, then shook his head. "Micah, even if she tells Piper no, you have to stay out of this. It's between the two of them."

"I know that, but I think she'd be really stupid to turn her down. A field of flowers just for her to use? How flipping wonderful is that?" Reggie nodded. "I can't believe that we were invited to come along as well."

"It's because in order for this to work, there has to be an agreement between everyone. And since you're in charge of the leap, that falls to you and I." He knew that, it had been explained to him by Pip. She'd been so nervous that he had a feeling that she thought he was going to turn her down. He looked over at Shane and Walter. They were talking quietly as he and Reggie were. "Do you suppose that they'll keep this to themselves?"

"I do. And Pip said that when the dragon comes to Shane, he's going to have help from the faeries too. I had no idea it was such a big deal." He hadn't either. The dragon had come as a surprise, yes, but what he was to Shane had made him scared. To have such a creature with someone so young all the time could be dangerous. "They'll be fine. We both know that."

He did on some levels, but a dragon? Micah wasn't so sure. Just as he was going to voice his concerns on it again, he saw a small light coming toward them and he watched it as it grew. Before he could warn the others that someone was coming, a woman, a beautiful brightly lit woman, stood in front of them all.

Her wings were huge, wide, and dragged along the ground behind her. There was light all around her as well, like a halo but not quite round. When she turned and smiled at him, he could see that her eyes, while bright like Pip's, were as clear as glass. When she bowed at them all, Micah had a feeling that she was as happy to see them as they were her.

"Hello. My name is Aurora, Queen of the Faeries and sister to all of nature. I'm so glad that we were able to meet tonight." Pip stood up and introduced them to the queen. Then she pulled Burke from his seated position and told her who he was. "Hello, young Burke Bentley. It is a great pleasure to meet you. How are you adjusting to all the new magic that is at your fingertips?"

"And I you, my lady. I'm getting the hang of it. Flying is fantastic, but having Piper as my mate is something that will make me happy forever." He bowed and smiled when he stood up again. "You have honored us by coming to see us. Piper has been planning this since she first thought of these plans of hers."

"I have seen them, and I too am excited. But I am also a little concerned. There are a great many others around that would harm such a venture. To have newborns at the ready, it would cause us a great deal of harm should it come to light what might happen here." Before he could tell her anything, Chris and Joey stood up. "The grand witch and her familiar. It is a pleasure, my friends. I knew who you were, but it is an honor to meet you finally."

"As it is for us." Chris put out her hand and an orb lit the area around them. "I have given my magic to this plan, my lady. The grounds will be protected by my magic as well as your own. This venture, as you called it, will benefit us both, I think. There is not enough magic…good magic…to go around. This will make it so much better for us all. It will be as safe as we can make it. The babes will never come to harm so long as I live. Any faerie here, they'll be as welcome as we can make them."

"Thank you, my lady. And this magic that you want more of? You mean the white magic of our kind?" Chris nodded. "My people, they have been diminishing over the centuries. The lands that we called our own are no longer as plentiful as they were before. Even the soil that we use now, it's not as strong. The flowers are just not like they were long ago. What makes you think that this will benefit us, Piper?"

"The benefit would not just be for you, my lady, but for me as well." Aurora stepped forward and put her hand over Pip's head. "I need this to keep me from harming myself and in that, others as well. I'm aware that to help me with my illness in any magical way would be a drain on you and the others, so this is what I am proposing for us all. I'm not saying that it would work, but I don't think that it will harm any of us to have more faeries. I have a friend that could benefit greatly from more of us."

"The holder of the dragon." Shane stood up and then bowed before the queen. "You have yet to meet him, yet you are as prepared as you would be a new day. That's good, young Shane. He will be your friend and ally for all your life."

"I'll be thirteen next year. In the summer, and that's when Pip said he'd come to me." He turned to his brother and Micah felt his pride of the boy double. "This is my big brother, Walter. While he doesn't have a dragon of his own, he protects me like he is one. Without him, I'd be dead."

"Not quite true, but close enough in your heart." Aurora looked at him and smiled. "You are a great leader, Micah Bentley. You and your mate have done well with this leap. I am proud to know you."

"And I you, my lady. My mate, Reggie, has helped me more than I can tell you." Aurora nodded. "You can't do any better than to have Pip in charge of this for you. She's a good person, and as my family now, she'll have all the help that she can use to make this work for all of you and your kind."

"I was thinking that as well." She looked at Pip. "You would do this for us? For no other reason than to help you."

"No. It would help all of us, not just me. And as much as I'd like to end my life nearly daily, I know that to do so would harm Burke and his family. Before them, before they barged into my life, I was alone in my decisions. Now there is them to consider as well. It will not end this need to end my life, but I have someone to help me with it." Aurora nodded. "The flowers will keep my head focused on them and not as much on my pain."

"You will take on a few of our people to help you?" Pip nodded and Micah could feel his excitement grow. "They will need to be with you. You are aware of this as well? And your mate, he is too?" They all turned to Burke when he cleared his throat.

"I'll gladly welcome them into our home, my lady. Piper has said that they'd take a little getting used to, but I'm looking forward to the challenge." Aurora laughed at Burke but gently so. "I promise you, I will. They won't be harmed by me or mine."

"Gladly welcoming them into your home will be something I think you will regret. Faeries can be a bit...well, you will see soon enough." Aurora turned to Pip. "I give you permission to do this for us. I will also provide you with the beginnings of the bulbs and seeds you will need to grow the best of them. When you have the first planting ready, I should like to be there. To make sure that what I have seen in your mind is what we get. I'm sure that we will, but I would still like to be there."

"You, and the faeries, will be welcome at any time." Aurora nodded, then moved to stand in front of Shane. She asked Walter to stand as well.

"You both should be rewarded. I know that you think you have done nothing to deserve it, but I think that you have." Both of them thanked her. "Shane, when your birthday comes and your dragon meets you for the first time, you will also be given a faerie. One that I will pick for the two of you upon meeting him as well. He will serve you both, my faerie, and make sure that you are forever safe from humans that would harm you both. For you Walter, I give this gift. It will serve you well over the rest of your life. The gift of memory. You will retain what you hear, see, and smell. A man who has been able to bring himself up from near ruin should have whatever he wishes. And an education is a profoundly wonderful aspiration. As I have said, I'm proud to call you my friends."

As soon as she left them a good hour later, Micah and Reggie made their way back to their home. Neither of them spoke of the things that they'd witnessed, but he was glad now that he'd been a part of it. As soon as they entered their home, he looked at his mom and grandparents, who had been waiting up for them.

"She's given them her permission." Everyone was so happy, his grandda especially. He wanted to help Pip with this project and anything else she set her mind to. "The queen, Aurora, is going to start them out with a few bulbs and some seeds. I guess they've been gone from this earth for a long time, but she's saved a part of them. Heirlooms, I guess we'd call them now. And once they're mature, Pip can start more seeds from those until they're as plentiful as anything that we have now."

"Oh, how wonderful for them all." His mom kissed him on the cheek and then hugged Reggie. "This is just wonderful news. But I'm off to bed now. This is so wonderful. And to think we're going to be a part of it as well."

Micah had been by the house today, the one that Burke and Pip lived in, and had fallen in love with it. It wasn't as grand or as big as his was, but it was lovely, homey, and suited his brother and his new mate very well. The greenhouse at the back of the property had been spectacular, and much bigger than he'd thought it would be. The number of workers that were there had made him a little uncomfortable. There were hundreds of small little people with wings working in every part of the huge place.

Micah made his way to his office. The need to unwind a little from all the excitement made him a little uptight. As soon as he opened his computer, he wished he'd gone to bed. The Masons had emailed him seventeen times since he'd closed up his computer at six to have dinner with his family. He noticed that Joey had been copied on them as well, and wasn't surprised that he called him almost as soon as he began reading the first of many.

"Do you believe this shit? He wants us to back off because we're ruining his vacation plans. The fucker should be in jail, not allowed to go away for two weeks. And what's to say he doesn't just not return? I'm going to make some calls in the morning." Micah just laughed at Joey as he ranted on and on. When he calmed, Joey asked him if he'd read them yet.

"Just the first one before you called. I'm assuming that they're not getting any nicer as he goes on." Joey said that was an understatement. "I agree about him leaving the country. We might not ever see him again should he do that. I've heard that he's taking his sons with him now."

"Yes. And so you know, Chris was able to find five of the twelve women that quit in the last few years." Micah thought that was a lot of them. "It is. And the five that we've found have had their attorneys call us. I don't know if they're going to play ball or not. I'm thinking that there might be some sort of settlement going on or something."

"You mean that he might have paid them off to shut them up. Sounds about right for him. You and Mason, you've butted heads before, haven't you?" Joey said that they had over a land deal a few years back. "That's right. You ended up with the house and now Garth has it."

"Right. That's the one." Micah laughed. "Yeah, Mason's not going to think it's so funny when we're done with him. He is going to get sued for slander if nothing else. He and his sons are saying some pretty shitty things about Shane. And that just won't do."

No, it would not. After they talked for a little while longer, they both decided that they'd table this for in the morning. Micah had to run into town for a little while and the two of them were going to meet for lunch. Their grandda was going to talk to his friend, Elroy, and he was going to meet them at his house for dinner. Micah was wondering what the man would have to say. As he was going up the stairs to his room, he thought of what the next week would bear. Thanksgiving, then the start of the holiday rush. He was looking forward to it this year more than ever with his new family to share it with. Micah loved being a father and husband.

~~~

Burke was making notes on the chart when he felt Piper's sorrow. He wanted to reach out to her, do what he could, but she'd told him the last time that he'd done it that she might only need a minute, that every time was not a crisis. It was to him, however, but he waited.

I'm all right. He told her he knew that. *I'm just having a moment. I think this was a mistake, taking this on. I'm not strong enough.*

Of course you are. You can plant whatever you want and make it grow. He knew this was true. Just before leaving for work today, he'd seen her put a single seed in the dirt and it grew almost immediately. When she was quiet, he told her about his day so far. *I had to put twelve stitches in little Tommy Cates's arm this morning. He thought that he'd use his new sled before the*

82

snow came. *Just to be sure it worked.* The stairs in his home are not as forgiving as the snow might have been.

Do you suppose his parents had ever done anything like that? He said that they had, as a matter of fact. His dad had been a friend of Tommy's father when they were younger. *How many stitches did his dad get?*

None, but a broken arm and grounded for two weeks. He'd broken more than his arm, I guess, and his parents were pretty upset with him. Piper laughed and he felt better. *My dad might have encouraged us to do something like that as well. He and grandda were forever getting their heads together and getting us into some sort of trouble. I miss him a lot lately.*

Your mom told me that he was murdered right around this time of year. He told her that was right. *She was telling me that he loved the holidays. I don't care for them so much. But your grandma assured me it was because I'd never spent them with this family. I suppose she could be right.*

The week after Thanksgiving my brothers and I get together to plan out our gifts. Of course you and the rest of the ladies are to come as well. We get Mom something big, then each of us get something to go with it. We were thinking a cruise with Grandma and Grandda this year. She told him that she didn't think she'd care for that. *Why not? I mean, it was something that she and Dad always wanted to do.*

And that's why I don't think she'd enjoy it. Especially now that she has grandchildren around. He'd never thought of her missing the kids. *I don't know what else you guys were thinking of, but I can see her going to an amusement park with all of you. Including the grandkids. I think she'd really enjoy that. Even if it's only for a few days. All of you in the same place without distractions? I think that's what she'd like.*

I think you might be right. Wonderful. We can bring that to the table when we all have dinner together. What about our grandparents? Any ideas for them? She said they would enjoy the cruise. *So long as there's food, my grandda would be thrilled. But Grandma would love that, I think. She's been hinting about it for some time.*

I have a little problem here. Not huge but.... Well, you remember me mentioning that some of the faeries would come to be in the house? He said that he did and was looking forward to it. *Well, I'm thinking you might change your mind. I came into the greenhouse a bit ago and there were several thousand of them there, all wanting to work in the big house, they call it. I'm pretty sure that other than their own homes, all houses are big to them. But that could be just me babbling.*

They want to live with us? All of them? He was trying to think what he was going to feed several thousand faeries when he thought of something else. *Will they be willing to share rooms? I mean, we have a large house, but I don't have any idea how we'd house that many, much less feed them.*

She was quiet on her end of the conversation, and he wondered what he'd said that was wrong. Yes, they would be crowded, but the house would help them out. When she spoke, he had to lay down his pen as well as push from his desk. His wings were tingling at the sound of her voice.

You would do it, wouldn't you? Put several thousand people in your home. He told her it was their home and he would do anything for her. *Thank you. But you should also realize that the faeries that I'm talking about are little. Like some of them, the taller of them is only about three inches tall. The rest are about one to two inches. They're faeries in the most basic sense of the word.*

Well, that makes it all the easier, right? When she laughed, so did he. *There is nothing in this world that makes me feel as good as your laughter does. Unless of course it's you screaming out my name when you come for me. That can make me feel like the man of* the world.

If I were to meet you in the woods tonight when you get off, do you think you could play with me? He reached down and adjusted his cock when it seemed to wake up. *This morning was much too fast. Don't you think?*

I think even if we were to make love for several days it would feel like it was much too fast with you. But I must admit, I love how you woke me up. Having you riding my cock was a pleasure to see first thing. She moaned, and he stroked his painful erection. *Why don't you come here now and let me show you how much I loved what you did to me? I could spread you out on my desk and have a tasty meal of your pussy.*

I'm so wet. He stood up and made his way to the door to lock it. He was going to be in too much pain if they kept this up. *What is in your office right now? Furniture, I mean. Do you have any chairs that are close to where you are right now?*

Do you want me to bend you over one? She asked him again what was near him. *Nothing at the moment. I'm standing near the door, and the closest thing to me is my desk, which is about four feet away.*

She was suddenly in the room with him. Burke pulled her to him, not even caring how she'd gotten there, because not only was she there, but she was naked as well. Kissing her mouth, he lifted her up to his body and took her to his desk.

"Christ," he told her as he sat her on his end of the desk and pulled his chair forward. "You're going to have to be very quiet. Last I heard there was a room full of people putting in the new security system out front."

"I've sound proofed the room." She opened her legs for him, putting her feet on the arms of his chair. "I can't wait until you make me come. I hope you don't mind that I came here now."

"Piper, whenever you can, you should just come here and let me have you. I would never want you to feel neglected." He slid his finger into her wet pussy and moaned. "You have to come this way for me. I want to see you when you do."

"You will if you keep that up." She rode his finger and he slid a second one into her. "More, Burke, I need you to give me more of you."

Leaning down to her pussy, he suckled her clit into his mouth and nibbled. When she screamed out her first of what he knew was going to be many releases, he fucked her harder with his fingers. Lapping at her clit over and over, he let his cat take him so that he could enjoy this treat as well.

His cat loved their mate. As he ate at her, lapping his large tongue not only over her pussy but her ass as well, Burke fell in love with her all over. His mate was special and he wanted everyone to know it. When she came again, this time laying back on his desk so that she could tug at her nipples and breasts, his cat nipped at her thigh before letting him take his body back.

Burke loved to feast on her. Her juices covered his chin and ran down his throat. The thought of fucking her after this, letting her taste herself on his mouth, made him want to stand now and bring her over the edge again and again while he fucked her. When she begged him to fill her, he stood up and fisted his cock. Stroking it over her, he watched her breasts as they heaved with need.

"Do you have any idea how much I'd like to spray my cum all over you right now?" He let his precum drip on her pussy then rubbed it over her clit. "To see your body branded by me is almost too much for me to think of."

"If you come on me, will you fuck me hard when you're finished?" He nearly yanked his cock off, he was so surprised by her words. "Come on me, Burke. I want to feel your hot cream when it touches me. Then fuck me."

He fisted his cock faster, watching her as she cupped her breasts over and over, tugging and pulling on her hard nipples until he wanted to beg her to feed him one of them. When she slid her fingers into her pussy, spreading her nether lips for him, he came then, his balls so painfully full that he had to hold onto the desk or fall over when he released.

Burke saw himself spray over her breasts, then her mouth and face. When she licked it, taking it into her mouth as she rubbed her hands over her cum covered body, he felt his cock stretch more, his balls fill again. And when she cried out, this time telling him that she was coming, he let his second climax take him. Again he covered her with his juices. They dripped from her chin, her breasts, even her navel. Burke wished he painted in that moment. Wished he could capture her like this for all time in art.

"Fuck me. Now, Burke." He didn't think he could, but when she wrapped her legs around him, pulling her to him, he slid his cock deep inside of her and leaned over her. Their mouths fused, it seemed, they were so hot.

His hands touched her, smearing his cum over her nipples and anywhere else he could reach. When Piper told him she was coming again, he slammed into her as hard as he could, moving the desk as he did so. And when she bit into him, tearing into his throat, Burke came again, his vision not just blurring but blacking out several times as he emptied into her.

Burke tried not to fall on her. He knew that he was heavy, but he was also weak. Even his knees were a little wobbly. So when she giggled, he let his body drop enough so that she could feel him there.

"I can take us home if you're not too busy." He started to

nod, then shook his head. "Well, that's too bad. I had more plans for your lovely body."

"Please don't. I think you might kill me if you did." She laughed again and he smiled at her, his strength coming back to him now. "I love you, Piper. So much."

"I love you as well." He wanted to make a big deal of her declaration, but he heard someone outside his door. "I think I need to leave you to your work. They need you out there."

"I wish we could do this more often." He stood up and was dressed as he'd been before, tidier and pressed, but the same clothing. "You do that well."

"You did it. You're getting better at this." Burke was going to have to talk to her about everything that had come with being her mate. "I have to get going anyway. There are a lot of things going on at the greenhouse right now." She went to the door and unlocked it and turned back. When she smiled at him, Burke felt the warmth of it deep in his heart.

When she left after a promise of a repeat whenever she needed him, he sat back at his desk. Christ, that was the most fun he'd had at work for a very long time. Smiling, he pulled up his first file and told the person at his door to come in. Burke was thrilled to death that Piper had told him that she loved him.

Chapter 7

Shane was glad to have Walter home again. He was glad that he'd been able to get into college, even applying as late as he had, but he missed having him around. Walter and him had grown very close since they'd come together as enemies. And now they were headed to the mall to get him a couple of things at the men's shop. Walter had grown another three inches in the last few months.

"I think because I'm feeling so good." Shane asked him how his classes were going. "Not too bad. But I have to tell you, when I pulled out one of my books to work on an assignment, I understood it a lot better. That queen, she really hooked me up."

"I'm glad. I was worried for you at the beginning of the year when you said that you were failing every class." Walter said that he'd missed them all and thought that had a little to do with it. "We missed you as well. And now that you have that car, we see each other a lot more. This is great."

"Do you think that faerie gave me that ability because she thought I was stupid? I mean, I'm not very smart, and I worked really hard to only get just barely passing grades so far." Shane asked him if he was serious. "Yes. I mean, look at you, all smart and all. You get really upset when you make a 'b.' I'm glad to make a 'd' in my classes."

"You're not stupid. And don't say that again. You just never had anyone believe in you before. And we do." Walter nodded. "Your parents never gave you a chance to figure things out, and you didn't know how to. You're getting it, and this thing she gave you, it's only jumpstarting what I knew was in you all the time."

Walter grinned at him, only taking his eyes off the road for a second. "You're the best, Shane. I know this sounds horrible, but I'm really glad that I had to beat you up that time. I don't think I've had a better friend than you." Shane nodded. While Walter had hurt him pretty badly, he'd also made it so that they both had a dad as well as a really great family. As they pulled into the mall parking lot, he thought of all the things he wanted to do while the two of them were home this week. They were joking around as they got out of the car, and were just crossing the road to the entrance when he saw something out of the corner of his eye.

The man came out of nowhere. As Walter was knocked away, Shane felt himself being lifted up and tossed away too. His head exploded in pain, and his arm and leg broke as he hit the pavement. He knew this because he could see bones sticking up out of his pants and shirt like someone had stabbed him with one. Shane reached for his mom and dad. Telling them where he was and what had happened, he felt his body being smashed again from behind.

We're coming. He told them to hurry, then thought of Pip. She didn't even ask him where he was, what was going on, she only told him to hold on.

She was suddenly in front of him. When she asked him if she could touch him, he screamed in pain and told her no. Then he saw Walter and told her to help him. He was laying in the road now, Walter was, and his entire head looked like hamburger. Shane was afraid. What if the person who had hurt them was coming back?

"Shane?" He opened his eyes, not even sure when he'd closed them. He felt odd, weak, and his vision was going in and out. And it was difficult to breathe well. "Shane, I've had someone call an ambulance. You have to listen to me. Can you do that?"

"Yes. I hurt." She said that she knew that but couldn't help him right now. "My mom and dad are coming. Can you stay here until they come? That person might come back."

"They won't." He wasn't sure what she meant, but he was starting to get sick from the pain. "When the police arrive, you have to tell them that you don't know what happened. That you and your brother were only going into the mall when you were attacked."

"That is what happened, then someone hit me." She nodded. "Then you came to help me. You told me that you could move faster."

"Yes, I did. But you can't tell the police that. They're going to wonder enough what happened to the men that hurt you. And why they were hit by a car." He started to nod, then stopped when his belly jumped. "Tell them that you hit your head and all you saw was the dead men. All right? You have no idea what happened to them other than what you could see."

"Car." He lifted his head up then. It cost him, but he had to see what she meant. "What happened here? I mean, they're dead."

"Yes, they are. Just the bad guys, however. Not the driver." Shane wanted to lie back down but was staring at the driver. "He's fine. I've held him in a trance so I could talk to you. Walter won't know a thing because he was out when I got here. Are you listening to me, Shane? You didn't see the car hit them. You have to remember that."

"Yes, I'll remember. Pip, I don't feel so well. I...I feel like I'm going to be really sick." He couldn't lift his arms or his head. He felt like he'd had the flu for a long time and needed to nap really bad. Shane closed his eyes and told her what he thought. "I don't know why someone would want to hurt us. We were just going to the mall for some new jeans. Pip, I really hurt and I can't see very well anymore. They were going to kill us, weren't they?" He couldn't keep his thoughts straight. His mind was buzzing but nothing was working right.

"No." That made him feel a little better. "Just you. Walter was just in the way. He'll be fine now, thanks to you. I don't think he would have made it had you not told me to look at him first. He hit his head pretty hard when they knocked him out of the way."

He didn't say anything. Shane wasn't sure he had the energy to breathe now. He heard the sirens in the distance and he looked up at his newest aunt. She was pretty. It was all he could think of, and she had the most.... She had wings. His mouth stopped working and he thought of talking to her.

I'm a faerie. You knew that. He heard her, but there wasn't much he could do to look at her again when his eyes just closed. *Are you afraid of me now, Shane? I'm sorry that you were hurt.*

I'm not afraid of you. But I'd really like it if people stopped trying to kill me. She laughed, and he felt his mouth turn up in a smile. *You should go now before they get here. They might question your having wings.*

They can't see me at all. Just you. Shane wanted to stop hurting and told her that. *Stay with me, Shane. If you pass out, your mom is going to kill me. She's pissed enough as it is.*

I won't let her hurt you. She said nothing, but he wasn't sure he could hold on much longer. *You saved my brother's life. I owe you for that. Pip, I don't think I'm going to make it. I don't know why, but I think I might be dying.*

No, no, you can't die on me, Shane. I need you in my life. Shane? Can you hear me? He told her that he'd give it his best, but he wasn't feeling good. *Shane? You stay with me. I can't fix you, baby. I'm so sorry. I should have touched you earlier. I don't have any more energy left to help you. Shane? The ambulance is here. You have to hang on for them. Shane, can you hear me? Oh, God, what have I done? Please, you can't die on me. Please. Aurora, I need you.*

Shane tried to hold on but he knew that he lost it a couple of times. Each time that he was brought awake, the men helping him would tell him to hang on too. He wanted to ask about Walter, but he hurt. Even his mouth hurt to try and talk any more.

Shane? He looked at the queen as she stood over him. *You're a good boy. I wanted you to know that.*

I don't want Pip to get into trouble. She saved Walter, but it's my fault that she can't help me too. I think I'm hurt more than she knew. She nodded at him, but he could almost feel her sadness. *She's not, is she?*

No, but she didn't have the strength to save you both. Your brother would surely have died had you not told her to take care of him first. Now...well, now you are in bad shape, and she cannot help you. Walter, his mind screamed at him, Walter had been hurt really badly, but he was going to be all right now. *She thought that you were in better shape than you were. And now it's too late.*

He died? She shook her head and then he got it. *I died. I was killed and I'm dead. Those men, they killed me. And because of her helping my brother, there was nothing or no one to help me, right?*

Yes, I'm afraid so. I'm so sorry. He nodded and felt the pain just wash away. *They're working so hard to save you, these men. Pip is helping them, at great cost to herself. She is draining her own body of magic to make them try harder to save you.*

She can't die too, my lady. Burke will be so upset and sad. I think there is enough sadness in the world now. Tell her to stop it. I don't hurt anymore. The queen said nothing. *You can make her, can't you? You can make her stop before she's dead too. It would be really sad if there wasn't a Pip in our family.*

Such love you have for mankind, my friend. I cannot let this go unrewarded. You're going to be fine, my friend.

He saw the bright light then, but it blacked out. Shane felt... well, nothing. He let his body drift away, feeling horrible that not only had he died, but that Pip would feel like it was her fault. He tried to make the queen understand him, but she was gone too.

~~~

Nolan wasn't sure where he wanted to be more. With Rylee or here beside the bed of his son. His son. Today it had more of a meaning to him than it ever had before. Holding onto his hand, he wasn't sure if he could hear him or not, but he spoke to him.

"I love you. I know that I say that to you a great deal, but I mean it. I'm so glad that you're going to be all right." He would need a great deal of rest, but Walter was going to be all right. "They said that you hit your head pretty hard and that it might be a few days before they know the extent of the damage if there will be any, but you're going to come home with us."

Nolan sobbed then. A normal outing for two young men had ended so tragically. Nolan let the tears fall as he held Walter's hand to his face, and sobbed all the harder for its warmth. He heard the door open behind him and didn't even bother to wipe his face.

"Son?" Grandda touched his hands, his work worn hands, to his shoulders and told him that he loved him. "I was just with Rylee. They're moving Shane from surgery now and into the recovery room."

"They should have been safe." Grandda said that he was right on that score. "Those men tried to kill my sons, and had it not been for Pip, they'd both be dead now. I don't know how I can ever repay her for what she did today. Ever."

"That girl, we owe her a great deal. When she wakes up, we're going to tell her that too." Nolan nodded. "I will sit with Walter here if you want to go with Rylee. She's down at Shane's room for when he comes out of that recovery room. She might need you there for a bit."

Nolan stood up and turned to look at his grandda. He'd grown old since this morning. Nolan felt like he had as well. When he hugged him, Nolan felt like he'd been blanketed in love, it was so powerful of a hug.

"You go on down there and tell him that we're going fishing soon. Even if I have to go out and have the ice pulled off by myself." Nolan nodded and pulled away. "Pip and Burke, they're not here, as you know. She's gotta rest up a bit more before she can...that girl saved him for us. Both of them."

Grandda sobbed with him. They didn't know everything that had happened, but they did know that Pip had saved first Walter, then Shane, by giving almost all of her strength to the medics that had come on scene.

95

Aurora had told them that the only reason that either of them were here and not gone was because of their sacrifice to each other. Both of them had said to give the other what they had left to save them. Nolan would forever be indebted to Pip, whether she liked it or not.

The Sheriff met him in the lobby and followed him to his son's room. Rylee had been devastated when she'd gotten to the scene. He'd been no better. He was glad now that Burke had been at their home when it happened and had driven them there, or he was sure that they would have been in some sort of accident too. As it was, he knew that he'd never forget the blood that had stained the concrete or snow that was pink with their life's blood draining away. But the sight of his sons, both of them, covered in their own blood, was something that he knew would haunt him for the rest of his days and beyond.

"I've come to talk to you." Nolan nodded at the sheriff, and when he sat down with them, the rest of his family joined them, all except Grandda, who was still with Walter. Whatever he had to say to them, he knew that he'd tell Burke and the rest when he finished up here. "I thought we could talk in private."

"They're my family and this is as private as it's going to get. If I thought that we could move this to my other son's room, where Grandda could be there too, I would." Sheriff Porter nodded and began. "Please tell me that you have something on those men. And that you know why they came after the two of them."

"I have some information, yes. They worked for Carter Mason. I know that you know who he is, but I just wanted to know if you've had any contact with him since.... I have to ask you where you were when this occurred." Nolan asked him what he meant. "When your sons were hurt, where were you, Nolan? You and Rylee? And who was with you?"

"At home. My family was there with me, our butler, I think some of the staff as well. When we got the call from the police, we were getting ready to leave the house to meet the boys in town for dinner." Which wasn't entirely true. They were leaving the house, but only because Shane had called them to him. "What's this about?"

"Carter Mason said you were threatening him, that you were on his front stoop when you got a call from the police. He claims that the men that hurt your boys were hired by you to make him look bad. He also mentioned that you threatened him with what went down and told him that it would be worth the death of your kids to see him fry." Nolan looked at his family, then at Porter again. "I'm telling you this because you're my friend. Not because I suspect any of this as being true."

"Have you read the report from the driver of the car? Do you have any idea how close both my sons were to death?" He nodded. "Then you tell me why I would hire someone to 'hurt' my sons to make him look bad when they nearly died? And you know as well as I do that I would never do anything to harm my family. They're my life. Christ, this is really wrong. On so many levels. Those men tried to kill my children, and you sit here asking me—"

"Nolan, that's enough." He looked at Rylee when she spoke. "I think it's time you left, Sheriff. We're dealing with a great deal of stress right now, and you coming in here and doing this now is not helping. Perhaps you should have a look at the dash-cam on the car that helped my sons out."

"We did. Everything that the driver says happened is right there for us to see. I won't go into any details, but you must know that as an officer of the law, I have to ask you questions or things could go south for everyone." Rylee nodded. "I'm sorry, for everything, but I want this settled as much as you do. And covering all of our asses is the only way we can make sure that all the parties are represented the same. You have no idea how sorry I am that I need to do this now, but I want you to know that I'm doing everything I can to make it so he can't leave town, not today as he plans. You know as well as I do what will happen if he does."

"I do and I understand." Rylee turned back to Shane as she continued. "And you have to understand that this means war."

No one said a word. Porter looked at Nolan, and frankly, Nolan was glad that someone had said it. This was going to get nasty now, and there was going to be blood. When Porter finally left them without another word, Nolan looked at his son.

Walter had been hurt badly before Pip had arrived. His neck had been broken, his head nearly crushed in. He had been alive, but only barely. There would have been no saving him even if the ambulance had been right there. Aurora had told them what Pip had done to save his life, how she'd used her considerable magic to mend him to the point where he wouldn't die. Now he was sporting a concussion as well as a broken arm. The rest of his wounds, superficial for the most part, would heal easily now. But not so much Shane.

"He spoke to her. Told her that he hurt but nothing more. He even lifted his head once to speak to her." Nolan had sobbed then, knowing that without Pip being there to call for more help, his son would be dead now. "She didn't touch him, not once. Had she done so she might have felt that his heart had been pierced by a rib and that he was bleeding to death on the inside. It wasn't until the medics got there and they rolled him to his back that she knew. But then...by then she'd been spent. But that didn't stop her. Even after she called to me to come aid her, she didn't stop draining herself."

"She gave her magic to the men there, didn't she?" Aurora told Chris that she'd given them more than she should have, much too much for her to have survived. "But she did. And so did Shane. What did you do?"

"Neither of them would let the other die. They were willing, both Shane and Pip were willing to give their lives for the other. Shane even begged me not to let Pip be in trouble for helping him. He said that it wasn't her fault that he'd called to her. Their love for one another, it's not like anything that I've seen in a very long time. It's as pure as the earth." Aurora sat down then, and smiled at them both. "It is something that we see so seldom in the magical world, a sacrifice so complete that they both would have died. I could not let such a thing go without reward. They both will...Shane will live to be as old as he wishes. And Pip now has more magic than she ever had before. I will not allow something like this to happen to either of them again. And Burke, he is just as magical."

"She's not going to be happy about this, you know that, right? She might even tell you to take it back. All of it." Aurora nodded at him. "Just so you know, I'm not going to be the one to tell her. I'm leaving that up to you. Or Burke. She won't feel that she deserves anything. I'm betting that she'll feel as if she failed us all."

"You're right, she will not feel as if she has a right to live." Nolan thought that was an understatement. He'd seen the scars at her wrist and had talked to Franklin about her as well. "Pip hurts more than any of you can imagine. Not just in her mind, but her heart as well. She *will* be...disappointed in herself to think that she failed young Shane in this. It has devastated her."

"She'll end her life. Or ask you to do it for her." Aurora said nothing to Rylee, but they all had known it was true. Piper would end her life somehow because she would feel like a failure for not being able to save his son's life. But she had, was all Nolan could think about then and now. Had Pip not gone to them and then called in the queen, they all three would have died there that day. Nolan looked at the queen again. "And this magic that you gave her, will it help keep her alive?"

"Yes. It will help. But she will need love, which I've no doubt that she gets here. And understanding. Something that she's never gotten and is not sure how to take. She needs this family more than you can know." Aurora stood up. "I must return to the forest. The faeries that were helping her, they are most upset. I will have to talk to them."

After she left them, Nolan reached out to Burke to check on Pip.

She's still resting. It's a kind of scary sort of rest. Her breaths are slow, so slow that I think that she's not breathing. Burke sounded so heartbroken that Nolan wanted to go to him and hold him too. *I don't know what I'll do if something happens to her, Nolan. She's my whole life now, and I just can't live without her in my life. I don't even want to.*

We'll do everything we can to make sure she knows how much.... Burke, *I still have my children because of her. I can't let her die for that reason alone. We all need her.* Nolan reached for Rylee's hand and held it in his as he continued. *As soon as she wakes up, bring her here, please? I'd very much like to thank her for what she's given us.*

You know that she won't feel that way. Aurora told me that she was going to be hurt by what she feels that she didn't do. Nolan told him that he knew that. *I've thought of the rest of what she told me too. About what she gave to both her and Shane to help them. Do you suppose it will help her be safe for me?*

He told him what the faerie queen had told him and of

the magic that they all received. Neither Shane nor Pip would die. Not by man nor magic of another being. The only people who could end her life would be Aurora or Chris. And he was positive that Chris would never agree to that. Aurora, he thought, would not harm what she loved any more than he would.

She'd have to have a good reason to want her to do it. Chris won't, no matter the circumstances. And Aurora won't either, not without a good reason. She is in awe of your mate, I think. Pip will have to petition to her with a good reason, but I don't know what her criteria might be. Burke said that if she did it, then he'd follow her. No matter what. *I figured you'd think that way. I know that I would if I were in your shoes.*

I love her. More than I ever thought possible. Nolan told him he did as well. *I can't stand to see her this way. I hate it with all that I am.*

I understand. I really do. I'm sitting here with my sons wishing it could be me in their place. I have never hurt so badly as I do for them. He looked at Shane with all his tubes and monitors on his small body. *Bring her here when she wakes. I think she needs to see what she's given us.*

Burke said that he would and they closed their connection. Nolan made his way to Walter's room to sit with him for a bit. He spoke quietly to his grandda about what Burke had said to him.

"I've been thinking on that too. And here is what I have come up with. Aurora said that the two of them are now connected with her. Both of them got some of her to live, right?" He said that was correct. "I think she should tell them that they're all connected. That they all share the same bond."

"They do, Grandda. I'm not sure where you're going with this." His grandda looked a little flustered, but Nolan knew that it was because he wasn't understanding him. Not because he was upset. "Burke is going to bring her here when she wakes up. I hope it will help her to see them both alive."

"She should tell them that they're all connected like one of them conduit lines." Nolan started to ask what he meant when his grandda laughed. "You know, one line is cut, they all don't work."

Nolan wanted to ask his grandda when was the last time he'd had his head checked out when it hit him. Yes. They were all connected. And if they worked this right, Pip would think, at least for now, that if she did anything to herself, it would affect the other two.

"Grandda, I think you have it. Now we have to figure out how to get Aurora to go along with us." Grandda said to leave it to him. "All right, but keep me informed. Okay?"

Chapter 8

Pip didn't want to move from where she was. She knew that sooner rather than later someone was going to notice that she was awake, but for now she was on her own. A lot of things swirled around in her head at the moment, mostly the situation that she'd failed at with Shane and Walter.

"They're both doing well. Walter woke earlier this morning, but Shane is still in a drug induced coma. They want to leave him that way for a few more days to make sure that he's able to handle the pain." Pip didn't move, hoping that Howie would just go away. "Not going to happen, I'm afraid. It's my turn to sit with you, and I'm not leaving until Burke returns from taking a shower. He was smelling pretty bad, and we told him to go and freshen up or you'd have a hard time being near him when you woke."

"I failed him. And the rest of you." He asked her how she'd

done that. "I had no idea that Shane was hurt as badly as he was."

"Happens. But in this case, it turned out well for him anyway. Had you not helped Walter, he would have died, I'm told. But he didn't die, thanks to your fast thinking. And from what I've heard, you saved Shane as well by giving those men and women there a little more of yourself to keep them going." She let the tears fall. "You can't be taking on the world, Pip, and expect to come out the winner every time."

"I can't seem to win at all." He asked her how she figured that. "I told him I'd keep him safe if he needed me."

"I said that to my son too. And as much as it pains me, and it does every day, I guess by your way of thinking, I failed him too." She rolled to her back and looked at him. "You think that just because you say something, something you fully believed, that anyone is going to think you failed them when you gave more than you should have to make it work? I don't think so. And if they did, then I'd like a word or two with them. There is no way for it to come out right every single time. Never. Heck, girl. Had I had my way, I would have gone down there that day and gladly traded my life for my son. Micah didn't deserve to die that day any more than them boys did being hurt. You have no idea how many times I wish I could have done just that and saved this family all that grief."

"This isn't the same." He asked her how it wasn't. "He was hurt badly. I could have given both of them some of my magic and they both would have been fine."

"They're both fine now. And as I've said, that's because of you." She rolled to her side again. "You thinking that because I'm not agreeing with you that the conversation is done? It ain't. I got me plenty more to say to you. So you just turn yourself right around here and listen to me."

She looked at him and felt his anger hit her like a slap in the face. "You regret me being a part of this family. You wish I'd never come here."

"If I wasn't a polite man I'd get up and smack you right in the face. What a thing to say to me. To me, who has been right there for you all this time. Even when you shoved me away like I was nothing more than an old rag." He stood up and she watched him, hurting for hurting him like she had. "Damn it, girl, you tore at my heart just now. And for what? To make you feel better about what you consider a failure? I got news for you, there ain't no failures in this family. Not a one. And you know something else? If there was someone who fell, not failed but fell, we'd all pick that person up, dust them off, smack them around a little if they needed it, and help them figure out how to fix it. You keep pushing us away and we come right back, now don't we?"

"I hurt." He nodded and wiped at his face with his handkerchief. "I don't want to live any more. I don't even know why I've been around for this long. I hurt so badly all the time, Howie."

"I know you do, sweetheart. I know. But do you know what will happen to you if you end your life right now?" She nodded. "No, I don't think you do. When you called in that queen of yours, do you have any idea what she did? Just to save your bottoms?"

"She had to save them when I couldn't." Howie shook his head and sat on the side of the bed that she was on. "I called her because I had nothing else to give them. I was spent and they were going to die."

"Yes, they were. Actually, she said that all three of you were as close to dying as she'd ever seen. But when she spoke to Shane about you, he begged her not to get you into trouble for saving him. She don't know rightly why he thought that you would, but he begged her to make you stop helping those medics with your magic. He knew, you see, that you were dying too. And he figured that he was a goner by then and there wasn't any reason for you to be too. You did the same for him." Pip nodded, her heart heavy with what Shane had done for her. "She said that she'd never seen anyone give so much of themselves, to sacrifice all of what they were for the other to live. It touched her, she told us, like nothing else ever had."

"She saved us all." Howie said that was about right. She'd done it for them. "She should have used all her magic on them. Perhaps then they'd be up and around, not in the hospital."

"I don't think you should be second guessing the queen, my dear. I don't know, but I'm betting she can be a mite testy about those sort of things." Pip smiled at Howie. The man was just too wonderful. "But since she did that, did you know that you're all connected as a person?"

"What do you mean?" He explained it like wiring in a house, cut one line and the entire thing don't work. "No, that's not the way magic works. She would have healed us all separately. And in that...no, I think you must have heard her incorrectly. We can't be connected like that."

"You see, that's what Micah said. I'm forever hearing things the way I want them, I know that. I do that because it's fun. Sometimes I get it my way, some I don't. And so you know, it was my plan to fib to you. To tell you that you were that way so you'd not try anything silly like, you know, ending that lovely life of yours. But when I talked to her, Aurora told me that she blanket healed you all, so that no one would have to wait on her help. I asked her if she meant what I said...had to explain it to her a wee bit. She doesn't have any electric where she needs it, but she got it." Pip shook her head. "Now don't be doing that. I'll think you are calling me a fibber. And while it was my intention to do that, I don't have to. It's true. You go on and call her here and ask her yourself."

Pip thought about it, but she wasn't sure that she really wanted to see her disappointment either. The queen had been good to her, and if she felt that Pip had failed too, well, everything that she'd done would have been for nothing. As usual.

"I been meaning to let you know about that greenhouse too. While you've been here lazing about, them workers have been busy. You should see them flowers they got all lined up in neat rows." Pip asked him how long she'd been resting. "Oh, going on about a week now. Scared us a bit, I won't lie to you. And I'll tell you something else about them flowers, I've been having me some fun too, going down there and helping them little guys out."

Pip lay back on the bed and felt her sorrow overwhelm her. But before she could be reduced to tears and the need to curl up into a ball, Howie took her hand. He held it in his warmer one for several minutes before he spoke to her. She loved this old man, as much as she did anyone else. His kindness was overwhelming but sincere.

"When my Micah was killed, I thought for sure that I was done too. Had me a place all picked out that I was going to do it to myself too. I'm betting you do too." She nodded when he looked at her. "Thought so. Sorrow and pain like that, like you live with all the time, it can make you feel and want things that you'd never want if you thought about the people that you were leaving behind. That's what got me up and going. My Katie, she needed me there. And poor Gracie. She was all set to do herself in too. Just leave them little boys behind because her sorrow and loneliness was too much. I got myself a little testy

107

with her...hated it, but I felt it had to be done. Told her that them boys done lost their daddy, what were they gonna feel like if she just up and left them too? And for no more a good reason than she was lonely. Now just look at her. Happy as I've ever seen her. Oh, I know she gets down, we all do, but them babies and you girls, you bring her right back up."

"There are days when I have to force myself to breathe. To eat, even to move out of the bed." He nodded. "I don't know what to do. It hurts so much. My heart and head hurt so badly from it. What if I can't move one day when you expect me to be somewhere? How will I explain to you that I just can't do it?"

"You say it just like that. I'm having a bad day, a meltdown, and I can't help you today. I might be better tomorrow or the next. I can't know how you do it every day. Not like you do, not daily, but I do know some of the pain you're feeling. And I'll tell you what to do, child, you come and find me or one of the others, and let us...whatever you need, you let us do it for you." Pip told him she didn't always know what it was she needed. "Yes sir, I can understand that too. You just ache with a pain so deep and so hot that you can't put words to it."

Pip nodded, no longer able to speak around the lump in her throat. Her tears fell freely now, much as his did. As they sat there, she realized that Howie might be the only person in the world who understood.

"When I was twenty, I got into a tub of warm water and cut my wrist. The first one was easy, just slice it open and let the blood flow. The second wrist, I nearly had forgotten it and had to work hard at staying awake to cut it. I know that I botched it up. For some reason I wanted a nice clean line." He lifted her sleeve up and looked at the cuts there. "I was alone in the house. No one lived there but me, so I figured I was...well, safe to carry out what I wanted to do."

"Something happened outside of your house and they needed to see you." She nodded at him. "Fates. They're a fickle bunch of women. I'm betting they saw what you'd done and were going to make you okay."

"There was a fire. Not at my place, and I've never been sure why they even broke into my home to check on me. There was an empty lot between my home and the one next to me. There couldn't have been any reason for them to think that there might be a fire in my house as well." Howie laughed and told her that she knew as well as he did. "I woke up in the hospital a few days later. My arms and legs strapped to the bed, an officer sitting next to me, keeping an eye on me."

"They were keeping you safe for my Burke." She didn't say anything but watched him. "They say that there is only one for each of us. One person to share our lives with, have a family with and so on. I used to believe that. I truly did. Then I saw what happened to Tony." She said he'd told her that he'd lost his mate to another. "Yes, that's about what happened. His mate was murdered by a man that had no more reason to kill her than them firemen coming to your home. Just the need to do so. And when it was all said and done, Tony was left with a hole in his heart that was almost too big for him. I'm thinking it might still be a little too big for him. But I also believe that he's not going to be left out of loving someone. I can't believe that. He's a good man and deserves someone in his life that can make his heart heal up."

"You think because you want it, then it should be right?" He asked her why not. "Because as you have pointed out, the fates are a fickle group of women. And things just don't work out that way just because you want them to. They might have wanted to do this to him just to see how he'd react."

"Nah, they'd never do that to one of their special ones." Pip asked her why Tony was so special. "Because he's a Bentley."

Pip waited for more of an explanation, but he must have thought that was a good enough reason. He was a Bentley, and to hell with any other reason. Pip realized in that moment that he honestly believed that what he said was right. That because they were Bentleys that everything would be just the way he wanted it. He was either off his rocker or completely right. She wasn't sure that he wasn't the latter of the two.

"Burke is coming. He's got it in his head that I should have called him when you woke up. I told him we had things to talk about, you and me." He looked at her then and she could see in his eyes something that she'd never seen before. Understanding. "We okay, you and me? You ain't gonna do nothing stupid now, are you? And you know what I'm talking about."

"Howie, do you always get your way?" He grinned and told her not nearly as much as others said he did. "No, I won't do anything stupid today. That's the best I can give you. Today you've dissipated all the monsters for me. I don't know what tomorrow will bring."

"Well then, I think I can take that. And then tomorrow when you're feeling a little down or a lot, you come on and find me and we'll talk again. I don't know if you know this or not, but I sure do have a lot to say."

"Yes, I have figured that out." He kissed her on the forehead and then stood up. "Howie, do the rest of them know what a special man you are?"

"I don't think they do. Some of them might think on it a little, but nobody says it right out to me. You keep telling them, darling, and maybe they'll come to see it too." He stood at the doorway until it opened and Burke filled the opening. "Now here is a man that can dissipate monsters. And he'll do it just for your love. Yes, siree, I think that you two are a match like none other."

Howie pulled Burke to him and hugged him like he'd not seen him in a week, rather than just a few minutes. To Pip he said that he loved her and that he was there for her. She told him she loved him as well. Then he was gone.

~~~

Burke didn't sit but got into the bed with her. Holding her in his arms, something that he'd done every night since she'd been brought here by Aurora, he closed his eyes and simply let the stress of all of this fall away. She was awake was all he could think of, awake and seemingly fine.

"I'm supposed to take you to the hospital as soon as you're strong enough. I think we both need a little more time, don't you?" Pip told him just not yet. "I'm okay with just holding you for the rest of our life. I was so worried about you."

"I killed those two men." He said he'd figured that out. "They were sent there by Mason to kill Shane. Walter being there pissed them off and they meant to kill him as well. They might have had I not called in the queen. She saved us all, Howie said."

"She said that had you not done what you did before she arrived, there would have been no saving Walter. And the magic that you gave the others kept them from giving up on him when by all rights, they should have." He knew what she was thinking, that he didn't understand because he'd not been there. Well, he hadn't but others had. "I can read your mind, remember?"

"I killed them before I had the driver of the car gun his engine fast enough to hit them both and kill them. I wasn't sure how that would look with two dead men there and two injured boys. I had to work on the dash cam too, just tweak it a little." Burke had also figured that out. "Mason wanted to make Shane pay with his life because he felt that he'd insulted his sons. I know this because he'd told the man that I killed first that no one was going to get into his personal life nor that of his family. What he did at home was only his business, but Shane had insulted him and his name. He had that man take care of a few other problems that he had as well. Other people are dead because of Mason and that man."

"You mean he had others killed in the name of his sons?" She told him that two of the women from his office were now buried in the foundation of the new parking garage, as well as a few other bodies that might shed some light on things. "Do you know where?"

"Yes. I saw it all." He held her closer to him as she continued. "His sons, one of them is just as bad as their father…Carter, his name is. The other…I can only find disappointment when I saw him in this man's mind. Like he's not as bad as the other. Their mother, not a nice person either, has it in her head that this family, our family, might be better off gone. She had the man looking for a way to introduce some poison into some of the foods at the shelter. She told him that even if all the vets down there had to die, it would be worth it to have the Bentleys out of their lives."

He thought of the lengths that these people were willing to go because of their children. He would do anything within his power, too, to keep his children safe, but not to the point of murdering over a hundred people to do so. Christ, this was bigger than they'd all thought. Well beyond that of a failed land deal that Joey thought it was about.

"I wish there was a way to get the police involved in this." She said nothing but got up and asked him where her clothing was. He told her in the bathroom. When she returned, she lay down again but handed him a small thumb drive. He took it and asked her what it was.

"The man—and I'm sorry, but I don't know what his name was. Most people think that when you read a person's mind, you know them. Not many people think of their names when they are running stupid shit through their heads." He laughed and she did as well. "The man, the one I killed, he recorded everything. Every conversation he had with the family. Not that he didn't trust them—he did completely—but because he had a memory problem and wasn't allowed to write things down. So he began recording things so he could write them down later. There are several notebooks at his home with all his dealings with the family in them. And because he nearly worshipped the Masons, he kept all kinds of shit of theirs. I mean, all kinds of shit."

Burke felt his mind roll this around. Christ, they had a list? Of all the things this man did for the Masons? He was almost afraid to ask the next question, but she answered him before he could.

"It's in his storage unit. Number fourteen at the Holiday Parkway exit. It has murder weapons, things that both men had used before, as well as things that Mason had him get rid of. Things I'm sure that Mason thinks he no longer has to worry about. This man, he liked murder weapons that had been used before, the blood staining them or the smell of the gun smoke still on them." She turned to him then. "You should also know that Mason has killed on his own as well. That this man had to take care of the bodies for him. In the unit there are maps and photos too, things that he went and looked at. Not just the two women that are in the foundation, but about half a dozen more too."

"And this man, Marty Roach is his name by the way, he

just left it out for anyone to find? The whereabouts of all this incriminating stuff?" She asked him if the police had found it yet. "Not that I'm aware of. So I guess that's the point, isn't it? He did hide it well, just not from you. He had a storage unit that no one knew about that has...well, everything in it. Seems sort of too easy, don't you think?"

"I find that usually things are easy. It's our distrust of it that makes it hard. As a people, we want things to be harder than they need to be, and usually make more work for ourselves because of it. It's all there, just like he left it." He thought she was right on that. "What do you think we can do with this? I mean, I can't very well go up to them and say, here I found this when I murdered those two men for you. I'm pretty sure that I'd get in just a little trouble over it."

"You're right, I'm afraid that won't work." He kissed her nose. "But I have a large family that has brain power of unimaginable magnitude. They'll come up with something. I'm sure."

When she rolled to her side again and let him hold her, he felt elated. He knew that she wasn't one to be cuddled or hugged, so this was a rare treat for him.

"Your family is good to you. And to me. I've never had anyone treat me the way that you all do." Burke kissed her neck and told her that he loved her. "I love you as well. I didn't think that I should, but I do."

"Why didn't you think you should?" When she didn't answer him, he rolled her to her back so that he could look at her. "Why would you think you shouldn't love me? Is it because you want to die so badly and you knew it would hurt me? It wouldn't hurt me, Piper. It would destroy me. I'd not be able to live without you in my life now that I've found you."

"Don't you see? That's the reason. I can't let you get hurt."

Burke

He kissed her and tasted her tears. When he lifted his head, he told her again that he loved her. "What am I going to do now, Burke?"

"Love me? Take care of me? I have to tell you, I think I need a lot of taking care of. You're so special to me. Did you know that? I think of you all day long, at the oddest moments. When I'm talking to a patient, I wonder what you would think of them. As I'm making notes on someone's chart, I find myself drifting to thoughts of you. Not always sexually, but there are times when I have to go into the bathroom and relieve the pressure in my balls or explode."

She cupped his cock in her hand and smiled at him. "You mean you get as hard as this? Or harder? I love it when you jerk off on me. It's so sexy."

"I'd love to do that now. Just stand over you and make myself come watching you play with all your wonderfully lovely parts. Then when I'm finished, I want to make slow love to you, bring you to peak several times before I fill you." He kissed her then, giving in to the passion that he could feel rolling over his body. "I need you, love."

"And I you." She pulled him to her and kissed him this time. His body was on fire for her. When he lifted his head and settled between her thighs with his body, she smiled up at him. "You are the best thing that has ever happened to me. You make me want to…no, that's not right. You make me need to survive. I'm not saying that I won't be taken under by my depression, but you make it easier to wake up in the morning and to deal with things with a different outlook."

"Because I love you. And no matter how hard or far you fall, you know that I'll be right here with you. Every single day, every step of the way. All of us will." She nodded and he kissed her again. "I love you so much, Piper Bentley."

Chapter 9

"Mr. Mason, the police would like a word with you." Carl put down his paper and looked over at his wife when their butler came in after a short knock. With a nod, she stood up to do what they'd talked about. They had figured this would come to them sooner or later. No one would touch his wife or sons, not as long as there was breath in his body. And if it came to that, he'd buy his way out of things to join them wherever they were.

As she made her way out of the living room, he stood up and straightened his tie. This would be over almost before it began as far as he was concerned. And those fucking Bentleys would pay for fucking up his evening. As soon as he was in a place where he could make a few calls, the Bentleys and their fucking goodness would be wiped off the face of the earth. Carl left his office and smiled at the two men there.

But they grabbed him by his arms, and he was tossed against his own wall and frisked just as he came out of the room and into the hall. They took not only his gun at his ankle but the one in his holster at his side. His wife was already cuffed and held by a woman in a uniform. She was sobbing when he snapped at her to shut the fuck up.

"Carl Mason, we have a warrant to search all of your homes as well as businesses. I'm also here to put you under arrest for the attempted murder of Walter and Shane Bentley. The murders of Sable James, Elizabeth Toby, Caroline—" The man droned on while Carl looked at the man standing beside him with his hand on his gun.

"May I call my attorney? I'm assuming that I'll need him to meet me downtown at the station again. He's not going to like being called away from his family on a lovely Sunday afternoon just to tell you that you need to let me go. You do know that you'll be losing your job over this one...what the fuck do you think you're doing with my sons? They're minors."

His sons were being led down the stairs by four men in suits. They weren't cuffed, but were being held by their shoulders, as if they were afraid they might run or something. Carl looked at Billy and could see that he was crying. Carter just looked defiant. And pissed off.

"Yes, they are. And these men are taking them into foster care until such time as a permanent home can be found for them. And I'm making you aware that their cell phones have been left in their rooms, as well as their laptops and any other electrical devices. As well as your passports, all four of yours. We'll be taking those and anything else that we deem necessary with us when we make a total sweep of your home and other offices." Carl looked at his wife when she sobbed that they were her babies and had done nothing wrong. "And you'll have to call your attorney when you're booked, I'm afraid. There is a lot going on right now, and getting you into custody is our number one priority. We can't have you leaving the country, now can we?"

"You mother fuckers are going to regret this. I'll make sure of it. Those Bentleys, they're behind this, aren't they? They paid you how much to come here? Whatever it is, I'll double it for you to back the fuck off." The man just laughed. "Do you have any idea who I am? What sort of power I hold in this town? I'm going to see that this little station of yours is done. Today if I can manage it. You just wait and see who is in trouble now."

"You have fun with that. And while we're talking about your money, the courts have seized that, as well as your planes. And as I said, passports will be coming with me. They've also taken control of the two accounts that you have overseas. It's been a lot of fun finding all the little loopholes you thought you had."

He was taken out to the cruiser and put in the back. His wife was put in another one. The cop turned to him as soon as he was settled with a seatbelt across his lap. "You have any questions for me, Mr. Mason? Ones that I can answer for you?"

"Yes I do. But for now, I want to know where you are taking my sons. I demand that you let me speak to them in private before you put them in harm's way. They're frightened, and I don't want them to be afraid that we're not coming back for them." The door was slammed in his face and Carl began to have a little fear touch him.

When he was left alone in the car, he began to make plans. First and foremost, he was going to get someone to take out the man responsible for this. He had no doubt as to who it was. Joseph Bentley and his fucking family. His attorney would need to be called, but he figured that when Milly called and

119

told him what was going on, he'd not have to call him as well. A hit needed to be taken out on this bastard right now.

It took them an hour to get back to him, leaving him alone in the back of the cruiser. With his hands behind him, he couldn't reach his cell phone or his keyring. The little key he had on it was made for this sort of situation, to unlock cuffs. It had gotten him out of more trouble than he could remember. His sons had ones just like it. As he struggled with trying to get his keys from his pocket, he tried to think what the hell they might have him on. Nothing came to mind. He'd covered his tracks better than snow did on a winter day. And it was beginning to feel pretty cold in the back of this cruiser. When the cop got in on the driver's side and his partner, no doubt his fuck buddy, got in on the other side, he decided to tell them just what was going to happen to them when he was finished.

"You think this is going to get you a big promotion? Well I got news for you, dumb fucks, you're going to be lucky if you can volunteer down at that fucking shelter they got downtown. A place, I might add, I'm working on having closed down. I have it on good authority that they don't have all the proper permits to have that thing running." The passenger cop turned and looked at him. "I want both your names and badge numbers. That way I can expedite your firing when I get to the station."

"I'm David Farmer. This is my partner William Burton. As far as badge numbers go, we got them, but if you just tell the captain our names that'll be enough for him. There are only twelve of us working there. He knows us all." Carl wanted to slam his fist in the fool's grinning puss. "You got any more requests before we head out?"

"Yes, I want you to take me to my wife. And my sons." He told him that wasn't going to happen. "Then I demand that you tell me what this is all about."

"I did. When I told you why you were being arrested. I can go over it again if you didn't understand me. And so you know, we're all wearing body cams so they know that we told you. And that when you asked, I said I'd repeat it. Do you want me to?" Carl just looked out the window without saying a word. "I'm going to take that as a no. Anyway, the list, I have it here whenever you need it repeated to you."

Carl tried to remember the names. Sable? No idea. Elizabeth? No. But just as he was ready to dismiss it as unimportant, he remembered a girl from his office named Beth. Big breasts, blonde hair, and a mouth that made a man beg to let him fuck it. She hadn't liked him overly much. Like that had stopped him, he thought with a grin. Then he remembered what had happened to her.

"Christ."

The cop turned and asked him what he'd said. Carl told him nothing and tried to think where her body had been dumped. He thought for sure that Roach had taken care of it, but for the life of him, if he'd told him, he had no idea. And now the man was in the morgue and couldn't be asked.

As soon as he got to the station, he was fingerprinted and his photo taken. No matter how many times he asked, he wasn't able to talk to his wife or sons, nor was he able to use the phone. Booking, they told him, as if that was the answer to it all

"Would you mind emptying your pockets, Mr. Mason?" He told the man behind the glass that he did indeed mind. "If you don't cooperate, then I'm afraid that we'll have to do it ourselves. And I assure you, you might enjoy it better if you just emptied your pockets onto this table."

"You're going to regret this." As he tossed his things on the table, he thought about the gun that the officer had taken from him at his home. "And I'll want a receipt for my weapon too. Don't think you can just steal from me and I won't say a word about it."

"We have it right here for you. Your gun, along with the rest of them from your home, are down at ballistics now being tested." His cock seemed to shrivel up and his balls tightened against his body so closely that he was sure that he'd not be able to walk well. "And if you'd like to come this way, we'll take care of you."

"I want my lawyer." He told him he could call him when he was finished. "No, you will allow me to call him right now. I'm sick of fucking around with you fuckers. Get me a phone."

He was, of course, ignored. As they took him to his cell, all he could think about was his gun and the last time he'd used it. Carl knew for a fact that the body he'd used it on wasn't going to be found, not for a very long time anyway. But he couldn't for the life of him remember if he'd used it before that problem had ceased to exist. Taken to his cell, he was told to dress in the orange jumper there and to give them the clothing he had on.

"I'm not wearing that shit." The man standing there looked like he might pull trees up by himself and just crossed his arms over his chest. "I'm not going to be here long enough for me to wear that nasty thing that probably hasn't been washed in years."

"Okay then. I'll strip you down and put it on you. Won't bother me none. I've done it before to men like you." He asked him what sort of man he thought he was. "Guilty."

In the end Carl pulled the jumper on. He didn't like handing over his suit and tie. It made him feel powerful to be dressed like a man. The jumper made him feel like a criminal. And he was most assuredly not one of those.

An hour later, after being fingerprinted, his picture taken, and a phone call, he was led to a room and his attorney was waiting for him. He'd meant to call someone in to do a job, but they told him, twice, that each call was being monitored and recorded. He wasn't sure that was right but called Benjamin instead. Without trying to imagine the people on the other side of the mirrors watching them, he told Benjamin Kline to get him the fuck out of there.

"I'm afraid that's not going to be possible. Not with what they have on you. and let me tell you, Carl, it's a shit ton of stuff. What the fuck were you thinking?" He asked him about what. Instead of answering him, he shoved a paper at him. It was copies of notebook paper.

"Where did you get this? This isn't mine." Benjamin told him that it was Marty's. "So? What does this have to do with me and my family? I'm telling you right now, they're going to pay for this. Did you know that they brought my wife in too? And my sons are in some sort of home or some shit. They're not the type of children who do well in poorer homes. They need the pampering that only their mother and I can give them. You tell them that. That my children need to be somewhere special."

"Your children should be the least of your problems, Carl. I'm aware that Milly is here too. I'm assuming that you want me to represent you both together?" Carl asked again for what. "In addition to having notes out the ass on every job that Roach ever did, he even recorded entire conversations that he had with you about certain jobs that you asked him to do. Your wife is also heard on the records, as well as your two sons. He royally fucked you over."

"There is no proof that it's even us. I mean, for all we know, it could be just about anyone." Benjamin shook his head and pointed to the papers again. Right there in black and white, it said that Roach called him Mr. Mason and his wife Mrs. Mason while he spoke to them. "Where the hell did they get this shit?"

"When Roach and his partner were taken to the morgue, they had their clothing emptied. Much like you did when you arrived here, but the police did it. And before you say it was planted, they have a very nice recording of each step in the process where they not only stripped both men of their clothing, but logged each thing they took from them. Then, with keys that were also on the body, they went to his house. There they discovered the keys to yet another place. A storage locker. With your name on it." Carl remembered Roach asking for a place to stash some shit. He probably should have asked what sort of things he was storing, but it was too late for that now. "There was enough evidence in that place alone to put you away for a very fucking long time. In addition to weapons with your prints on them, blood stained clothing, and a shit storm of other things, they found the notebooks. Page after page of shit about you and the jobs that you had him do. It looked as if he transcribed each and every one of them."

"No, he'd never do that to me." Benjamin told him that not only had he done it, but he'd implicated his family as well. "What the hell are you going to do about this? I pay you a lot of money to keep me looking good."

"You want my advice?" Carl told him he did. "Confess to it all and try and get a lower sentence. It's the best you can hope for, a long stay at some prison instead of the death penalty. Because as it stands right now, that's what you and Milly are both looking at."

"On what charges? A man's doodling in some book? You have got to be kidding me." Benjamin told him that he was not. "There is no way that this is even going to go do court. You do something about this. Right now."

"What? You tell me and I'll get right on it. Legally. Because from where I'm sitting, the most you're going to get me to do for you is sit next to you while the prosecution tears you apart." Carl leaned back in his seat and asked him what they thought they had. "You don't think them having the murder weapons is enough? Christ man, they have you holding the smoking gun. What is it you think you can do to get out of this? They have your weapons."

"What weapons?" He told him. "No. No. No. They can't have anything like that." Carl leaned closer. "Those are no longer around to be used against me."

"You should have checked better. As it stands right now, they not only have each and every weapon used, but there is a tag on it with who the person was that used it, when it was used, where the body is, as well as the reason they're dead. They fucking have everything but you saying you did it. And that, my friend, isn't really necessary at this point." Benjamin stood up with his briefcase in hand. "Confess. Both of you. That's the advice I have for you. If not, you're going to die at the hands of the state."

"I didn't do anything wrong. They can't do this to me." Benjamin nodded and went to the door. "Where the fuck are you going? You have to help me."

"You're fucking right about that. I don't have a choice. When I petitioned to be taken off the case for reasons too numerous to list, I was denied. The judge said that I'd made my bed with you, I'm going to have to go down a merry path that you created for us." Carl asked him why he'd want to be off the case. "Because as much as you sit there and say you're not going to prison because they can't do this to you, I can tell you that they can and have. The question you should be asking yourself is which one. Not whether or not they can make you go, but where they send your ass. And Milly's. You two are as good as there now. Do what I said, Carl, the same thing I'm going to tell Milly. Confess. It might be the difference between you dying or living."

When he was taken back to his cell, all Carl could think about was that this wasn't right. That he had things planned. His life was mapped out, and that did not include him going to prison. Who was going to train his sons to take over for him? Who was going to turn them into men like their father? People were going to pay. And pay they would when he was finished being dicked around like he was.

~~~

Pip moved down the row of trays of dirt. It had taken her the better part of the day to figure out how to get things organized in a way that there weren't two hundred faeries under her feet. And in her hands. She looked over at Etran when he cleared his throat.

"What is it now? I told you that she wanted them done this way." He nodded but still said nothing. "Tell me please? I've a terrible headache and you're not helping me."

"The others, the little ones, they want to help you." She nodded and looked up at the ones she'd told to leave her alone. "They think that if you'd just let them go from your command, they could find other work that would not vex you so."

"I wasn't vexed, I was pissed." He nodded and grinned at her. "Tell them that I need some peace right now. I'm not used to so much going on at once. If they could...I don't know, just do things without causing such a commotion, I could handle it."

"They wish to please you." She knew that too and felt the tears fill her eyes. "Do not cry, my lady. 'Tis not your fault that they're noisy and nosey about things. I told them to go gently with you, that you'd been drained. But they want to help you with that as well."

"How?" He looked up, then back at her. "You mean to let them come and touch me again? I told you, it was too much. They were.... Did you see what they were doing to me?"

"Yes, my lady, I did." She wanted to stomp her foot but was afraid of making them scatter again. "You should just tell them what you want. With a calm voice. They do not care for screaming any more than you do them touching all of you. I think you might have frightened them a little too much for the first time here."

She looked up, and apparently that was all the invitation they needed to come down to where she was. As they sat down on the bench she was working on, she had a single thought. They were there to hurt her. She had no idea where that thought came from, but it felt as true as anything else in her life. As she backed from them, suddenly overwhelmed again, she saw Etran fly to be in front of her face.

"Just breathe, my lady. Breathe for me, and we will get things organized for you." She nodded but couldn't seem to let the air building up in her go. "Let it out, my lady, then suck it back in. Over and over until you can speak. We can wait." And he did, as did the others, all of them sitting quietly on the bench.

"Yes, all right. I'm sorry." She did as he asked, inhaling and exhaling several times until she was ready to face them. They were so eager, that was the problem. That and she wasn't used to hordes of people. She decided to just empty her thoughts to them.

"I'm nervous. And I don't want to mess this up. The queen thought this was a good idea and I feel like if it's not right, she'll be disappointed in me." Etran told her she was doing fine. "I don't feel like it's going any way but terribly. I don't even know what I'm doing."

One of the faeries stood up and walked toward her. "My name is Prisane, my lady. And I've been taking care of the flowers around the woods for a great many years. If you do not mind me pointing something out, you are planting them too shallow. May I show you?"

Pip stepped back and the little faerie stood in one of the many trays that she'd planted. When she stomped hard on the dirt, Pip could see that the seed did go down deeper into the dirt, almost to the bottom of the tray.

"It says in the instructions on the Internet to plant them only about an inch deep." Pip pointed to the information that she'd printed that she'd found yesterday. "And to water them when I've got them in the soil."

"These are not seeds that come from a plant store, my lady, but seeds that we have nurtured ourselves to be replanted. Seeds like this, very old ones, they need more dirt to make them grow better. The bulbs too." Pip looked over at the mountain of bulbs she'd not even touched yet. "If you were to fill the pots for us, we could put the seeds as well as the bulbs in the soil at the right depth, then you can cover them for us. Even Etran has a way to make that go faster. We all do, but not like he does. He's older."

She looked at the faeries that had come to help her, all of them so happy to be here. Pip wanted to tell them to do it themselves, her depression taking her breath away at feeling like she'd failed, but she let out a long breath and nodded. One step at a time, Burke had told her. Just do one thing at a time and it will be all right.

Pip and Prisane worked for nearly an hour on just getting the right amount of dirt in the pots for the bulbs. Once that was figured out, how much to put in, the way it had to be loose in the pot as well as how the bulbs would be covered when they were planted, she moved to the trays of dirt to watch them work. With the smaller trays of dirt, they were able to work the dirt in with the seeds without her help. Pip marveled at how quickly and how efficiently they were working.

Going back to the pots, she came up with a system, with the help of about a dozen more faeries, and had over two hundred colorful little pots with equally brightly colorful flowers in them filled by the time she was ready to call it a day. Standing up, she felt every muscle in her body protest.

"I'm not used to this sort of work." Etran laughed when she did. "Thank you for today. I should have listened at the first and we might have gotten a good deal more done. It was kind of you to take me to task. I thank you for that."

"It is fine, my lady. What we have done now won't have to be done tomorrow. And once you put your magic to what we did finish, we will have plants to show the queen tomorrow." She wasn't sure how to do that either. "Ah, you are new to this as well. Here we go. I'll walk you through it."

By the time she had spread her magic to all the trays, she was exhausted. But she was also feeling really good about what they were doing. By sometime tomorrow there would be blooms coming up. And of those blooms, she was going to take half of the plants to the shop in town. Hopefully they'd be able to sell even half of them.

"You should do it yourself." She asked Prisane what she meant. The little faerie and her brother Etran had decided that they were her assistants, and that suited her just fine. "Have a shop in town, one that only sells plants and trees. We could help you with it. There are no places in town to buy pretty bulbs, not like you have."

"You mean a greenhouse that sells plants? I wouldn't know

the first thing about that." Prisane said nothing as they locked up the building. There was an opening at the top for the faeries to come and go should they want, and she'd put out cotton for them to use to sleep too. She thought again about what Prisane said. "What makes you think anyone would want to buy plants from me?"

"Because you are faerie too." That seemed to be the only answer she felt that Pip needed. "I must go and attend to my other duties, my lady. And do not forget to ask the leader if it would be all right with him that his daughters have someone with them. I should like to know what his answer would be."

So would she. Pip wasn't sure after today that she'd recommend anyone to have faeries around them all the time. For the few hours that she'd had to work with them, she'd found them to be annoying. Then she smiled.

"Perhaps it was all me." She'd been nasty to them...she knew that now, but they had only done as she'd asked. And maybe they'd not be too bad with just two of them. They had pointed out that young Shane had a dragon now as well as his own faerie, and that Walter too had someone to watch over him. To keep them safe, she'd been told. As she headed in the house to get ready to go into town, she wondered what the big man would say to their request. Pip figured he'd say no.

Chapter 10

"And they'd just be there? All the time with them?" Burke had to put his hand over his mouth to hide the smile. It was harder and harder for him to even stifle the little laughter that spilled out. He thought for sure that Micah was egging Pip on to see her lose her temper. "How would we feed them? Where would they sleep and shower?"

"As I have told you, several times now, they eat very little and would take care of it on their own. They would sleep in the crib with the babies. That's how they would keep them safe. And if they need to shower, maybe they'll join you in your own bath. They could hang out on your small dick while you bathe. I'm sure that one of them could find some room on it even if you are erect." She glanced down at his cock and seemed to find it lacking.

Grandda lost it and was leaning over laughing. Grandma

had tried hard to look shocked, but she, too, was laughing. Even Reggie had joined in on the fun when Pip had finally had enough.

"I'm sure I have plenty of room, erect or not, for any and all your little friends." Burke started to tell his brother that he was wrong about that when Pip went to the window and opened it. As she gave a shrill whistle, Burke backed up. He'd seen her do this before.

The room seemed to shrink when they came in. Every one of the faeries, all the colors of the rainbow and then some, filled the large room. None of them touched the other occupants of the room, but moved around with their wings beating hundreds of times a minute. Burke was very careful where he stepped as he made his way to Micah.

"You were saying?" Micah looked shocked, and not only that, but a little frightened. He didn't blame him when they were in force like this. They were a little scary, even for their size. "She's been under a lot of stress, and when she calls them to her, they come. You might want to remember that the next time you try yanking her chain."

"I will. Are they harmless?" Burke shook his head slowly. "You do know that they're only about two inches tall, right? How bad can it be?"

"They do everything en masse. Yesterday I saw them lift a hundred-pound bag of soil and move it across the room like it was nothing. When they work together, they are impossible to stop." Micah looked at them now, all of them, as they moved around his living room. "When your children are in their care, you can bet that they're safe."

"I think you might be right." He looked at Pip and so did Burke. Christ, she was beautiful standing there with the small faeries all around her. "Burke, she's scary herself. I don't mean like monster scary, but just plain scary."

"You know it."

After that, Micah not only agreed to have the faeries watch over his children, but he also decided that he'd like a few of them in his house, if it was all right with Piper. Micah also begged her to forgive him for being an ass.

"You are an ass, but you should also be aware that they're watching over the Masons too. Not just the boys, but the husband and wife as well." Micah asked her why they were doing that. "Because they hurt my family. And if they get out of line again, I won't be able to stop the faeries from harming them. As Burke told you, when they are of a single job, they will kill anything that they deem a problem."

"Would you? Kill, I mean, if you found a problem too much to bear?" Piper only looked at him when Micah asked. "I see. And should we be aware of anything else?"

"Yes. But I'm pretty sure everyone knows by now. You're a dickhead." Everyone laughed again, even Micah. As they headed out the door to go to the hospital, Burke thought that he'd give anything to see Piper this happy all the time. He was glad now that his grandda had talked to her.

The ride to the hospital was quiet. Burke had gotten them a new car each, but they were riding in his at the moment. She didn't drive yet, but he was going to let someone else teach her. Perhaps Reggie or one of the other women. He'd heard that you never wanted to teach a spouse how to drive or work on a car. It could mean the death of you.

"I was wondering about something that Prisane asked me about. I don't want to do it at the greenhouse at home, but in town. A nursery, that sells the things that we grow. She pointed out that when we sell them locally to the other shops in town, we were only making about half. Not that I want to charge too much for them, but it might help defray some of the costs of soil and fertilizer." He started to point out that the queen was giving them some of the things when they needed them. "She said that with the income we could put it in an account to buy more land for them. To plant the flowers and to start growing trees so that they can enjoy them for as long as they wish."

"My grandda has a couple of buildings downtown. I bet he'd love that idea too. He's forever trying to drum up more business. And when you were resting, I think he loved working with the faeries for a while." She nodded and looked out the window without commenting. "Do you want to do this?"

"I think it would be a good way to take care of them, as she said. But I can't work it. I don't care for being around people that much. Do you suppose there is a way that we can get some of the people from the shelter to run it and work it? I mean, we could do the scheduling and buy whatever is needed to make it work, but I just can't do it." He loved the idea and told her so. "I know there are some things that go with a nursery that we can't grow. You know, like pots and soil. I went to this one a long time ago that also sold things for faerie gardens. Fake ones. Haston, he's another faerie, he said that most of them make their own furniture and would love to make things for the fake gardens for people. Here, let me show you what he meant."

She dug into her pocket and pulled out a little box. He'd meant to ask her about it earlier, but when she pulled out little tables, a swing set, as well as the smallest blankets he'd ever seen, Burke pulled over and looked at them.

They were well made, mostly of twigs and stones, but the detail on them was astounding. He set the little bench swing on the dash and pushed the little seat. It went back and forth much better than the one he'd had put on their own deck. And it was prettier too. Burke picked up the small table when she set it down. There were seed hulls for plates, smaller twigs for cutlery. And even a tiny vase with greenery in it for the middle. He was so excited that he hugged her three times before talking.

"The customers will love this. I do too. Can you see this, in a large pot with some moss as the grass? I mean, really, this is amazing work. And people will eat it up." He handed her back the things and merged into traffic again as he continued. "You show my grandda this and he will be trying to get you to start it now, like today."

By the time they got to the hospital, he had it all worked out in his head. Not the building—he knew that his grandda would help her with that—but how he was going to just let her do it. At first it had been in his head to tell her how to do it. Take over, in other words. Like he had any idea how to run a business that didn't have medicine or patients in it. She would make this work, if for no other reason than the little ones would need it too.

Walter was sitting in his bed, but he was still pretty weak and banged up. The tubes that had been helping him as much as the drugs that were still being given to him were all gone. He smiled at them when they all converged in his room. Rylee held his hand in hers and told him how much better he was looking every day.

"Yeah, I just bet. They let me have a look at myself today. To shave and brush my teeth. I think I look like a zombie or something. I even got to eat real food this morning. If you count oatmeal as food." They all laughed. "I asked after Shane. They won't tell me too much other than he's still in a coma. Will he make it? That guy, I'm telling you, he is the best brother anyone ever had. I just can't stand the thought of him being hurt like we were."

"He's still in the coma but expected to make a full recovery. As a matter of fact, they're going to start to bring him around this afternoon. We wanted to come and see if you felt up to going with us." Walter told him that he would even if he was hurting. Rylee smiled at him, her tears flowing freely. "I'm so glad that you're going to be all right. You have no idea how worried I've been."

"Me too." He kissed her hand too and looked around the room at them all. "I have to admit one thing though. I wish that I could have had my first Thanksgiving with you all. It breaks my heart to know that I was here and you were enjoying all that food. We never did anything much but yell at the cable company for turning off our service when the game was coming on."

"We didn't have it yet." Walter asked Grandda what he meant. "None of us wanted to miss having it with you and Shane either, so we just put it off. We can feast when the two of you are home where you belong. And let me tell you, it's going to be the most thankful Thanksgiving we had in a coon's age too. I even get to have all the pie I want."

"I never said that, Howie. I said that you could have a little extra in celebration. That does not give you license to fill your belly until you pop." Burke watched his grandparents and thought if there was a truer love, he had no idea how it would have worked. They loved each other so much, it was as plain as the noses on their faces. "I swear there are times when I think you like making me mad. Do you?"

"Now why would I do a fool thing like that?" Grandda kissed Grandma on the cheek. "You're the best, my love. A man could live a long time on just being around you all the time. It's what keeps me happy."

"You're a sap." But Burke could tell that she loved him.

Hell, he didn't think his grandda had a single enemy. His grandma kissed him too. "But I do love you, you old turd."

They helped Walter into his wheelchair. It was tough going for the young man…he was still hurting, but he was determined to go and see Shane. As they crowded in the room where the doctor already was, Nolan and he looked over the chart. They'd been doing that since the boys had been brought in, and knew they were getting the best of care.

"We're going to do this slowly, over a period of an hour. And as we discussed, if it looks like he's in too much pain, we'll stop there. I want him awake as much as you guys do." But not for the same reasons, Burke thought. They wanted their little guy to be all right. The doctor wanted to see what sort of, if any, damage had been done to him. When his rib had punctured his heart, there had been damage done to his lungs too. That was why they'd called in Barron to help out.

"You do know that this will mean that I have a connection to him. One that can never be broken but for death." Burke had nodded. "His dragon, he will not like that a vampire will be a part of them. Someone will need to explain that to him, or I will die the next time I come to see him. I shall be most upset if that happens. I care greatly for this family."

"And we do you. I'll have someone talk to the dragon on your behalf. I don't have to tell you that we owe you for this." Barron had said it was him that would forever owe them, but they parted on good terms, and Shane had taken a good turn because of the powerful blood in his body.

As the time slowly crept by, Burke was careful not to get his hopes up. Shane opened his eyes at one point and looked at Rylee. Then when he closed them again, he smiled. It wasn't a perfect way to see that he was going to pull through, but it was hopeful. Burke watched the doctor too. He would give away so much with just a look.

But as far as he could see, he was just as pleased at the rest of them. Burke let out a long breath that he'd been holding. The kid was going to be just fine, he knew it.

~~~

Carl was sick to death of being treated this way. He was in a fucking cell that looked smaller than his first car. And the bed was shitty. The food was horrendous, and not nearly enough. Even if he thought about eating it, which for the most part he did not, Carl thought there should have been at least a menu that he could pick and choose from. Just because he was in a fucking jail cell, there was no reason to treat him like a fucking criminal. He looked at the mirror that hung above his cell in the long hall when he heard the door opening. Carl could see every move anyone made coming toward him.

This particular cop was a fucking idiot. Carl had started calling him Barney, from that old black and white show from the sixties. As he whistled, the sound of it grating on Carl's nerves, he swung his keys on his fingers like it was an Olympic sport and he was going for the gold. Carl hated everything about the man.

"Mr. Mason? You in here?" He asked him that every time he came down the hall. Where the fuck else would he be, he wanted to ask him. "You got yourself a little message. I got it here if you want it."

"Of course I want it. Give it to me." Barney held it to him with a cocked brow, as if he were waiting for something. "Well? What are you waiting for? Give it to me now."

"Don't you know the magical word?" Carl wanted to tell him it was *fuck you*, but he'd never see the note if he did. The man was going to die soon if Carl had anything to do with it. "What do you say?"

"Give me the fucking note now, please?" The man grinned but didn't turn it over to him. "I swear to Christ I'm going to hurt you when I get out of here."

"You think so?" The officer handed him the note, but in his greed to get it, Carl tore it in half. "There. You see what happens when you get all uppity and nasty with someone? Now you're not going to get the full meaning of the note from your wife."

"My wife? What is she doing writing notes to me?" Barney just shrugged. Carl tried to piece the note together, but there wasn't going to be any reading it. "Do you know what it said? I'd really like to know what my wife is up to with this."

"She said that she's got herself an attorney." He asked him why he'd care about that. "Don't know. Could be on account'a you being brought up on other charges that she's sure she ain't got nothing to do with."

"Who the fuck has she been talking to without me there?" Barney just laughed. "I demand that you bring her here to me this minute so that I can tell her what she's to say. I won't have her going behind my back and telling you idiots things that she doesn't know anything about. And you were told to bring me my sons for a visit. Where are they?"

"First off, I'm not an idiot. I give you the appearance of being one because it gives me a giggle or two. Secondly, you are not going to have your wife brought anywhere near you until the judge says it's fine and dandy with him. And third?" He grabbed him around the throat and lifted him from the floor. "Third? You are never going to see the light of another day if you don't back the fuck off with giving orders to people. We are on different sides of the cell now, bucko, and you'd do well to remember that."

When he was tossed back, Carl held his throat and felt the burn of it all the way to his feet. As he watched the man standing there, Carl saw him go from educated man with an iron grip to the hokey he'd been portraying all along. The transformation was quick and complete.

"Now, for your boys. One of them, I think his name is William, is in juvenile detention. Seems the apple don't fall far from the tree with that one. The other one, Carter, he's in a home with some very nice but strict people, who are not only making his ass work for his supper, but making him toe the line as well. He'll be a better man, I think, than his father or brother can ever imagine." Carl asked what Billy had done. "Tried to kill Carter."

As he walked away, Carl wasn't sure if he was proud or upset with his oldest son. Carter had always been more of a follower. It was what got the two of them into trouble as a unit all the time. Billy would think up the plan, execute it, and Carter would stand and watch. But they'd be there together, so they'd get punished by whatever hard ass that was there trying to stifle their creativity. Billy was his son all the way. Carter...well, if they'd been born at different times, he might have thought that the boy wasn't his at all. Hell, he didn't even act like his mother most of the time, and she was a real bitch when she wanted to be.

Thinking about his wife, he wondered what she'd been told. Or if she had figured things out. Carl had done some things that would get him into some deep shit if anyone ever found out. He didn't regret them, not really. He'd wanted things done a certain way, and if they didn't go as planned, he made sure that those around him knew he was upset. But she might have found out about the women.

There had been a lot of them over the years. At first he'd only paid them off. Giving them baubles if they wanted them, cars or homes. Then he realized how stupid that had been.

Leaving them around to tell others, his wife especially, what he'd done to them. Carl then was introduced to the date rape drug.

Carl had never cared if his partners participated in sex with him. He liked it, as he did his business dealings, to be his way. And sometimes, most of the time really, the women would get all pissy about some of the things he'd done. So what if they had a few scars and burns? It was not like they didn't get something out of it. They had been fucked by Carl Mason.

But the drug, that had opened all kinds of doors for him sexually. The first time he'd used it on a woman, he'd fucked her for over two hours. Not just with his dick, but with anything he could put his hands on. Christ, he was hard just thinking about it. And the blood on her body had been such a turn on, he'd taken pictures. He'd jerked off to those for months before he found the next fun target.

Beth. That had been the name of the broad that had not just turned him down, but had threatened him as well when he'd asked her, politely he thought, if she'd suck him off for the raise she should have had anyway. The little cunt had told him that she was going to report him to his wife. Not really a big threat, that. His wife had more affairs than he had. And then she was going to go to the ethics board at his own fucking company. What the hell had she been thinking? That he'd just tell her, okay, go for it?

So he got her into a meeting with him, to discuss plans to settle the problem she had with him—as if that was ever going to happen—and he'd drugged her. Plain and simple. Then when she was out—well, not really out of it, but enough that she knew what he was doing to her but unable to say anything—Carl had fucked her, then let three of his buddies have a good time with her as well. One of them had even taken her lovely tight hole and had made a carving in her pretty ass while he'd done it. Carl had gotten off on that twice while he watched. Then when they were all finished he'd strangled her to death as he fucked the life right out of her. Christ, it had been the best he'd ever had, before and since then.

Carl had never thought of himself as a sadist. He supposed that he was. But he was a lot more too. While he didn't like to be in pain himself, he really enjoyed inflicting it on others. And while he did enjoy a good vicious fucking, he didn't want anyone to tie him up or his victims. He smiled then; victims... such a lovely word for the women he took. He wanted this shit over with so he could go out and have some more fun.

But now here he sat with murder charges pending, and he had no idea where any of the bodies were. Literally. He knew that some of them were in the foundation of a couple of buildings, Beth being one of them. As for the rest? Nope, not a clue. Carl had read somewhere that without a body, they had no case. Well, as far as he was concerned, he was out of here the first time one of them stupid Bentleys tried to say he had done anything wrong.

He looked at the torn note again and picked up the pieces. There had to be more than whatever Barney was spewing. Besides, what else did he have to do while he waited for his attorney to get on the stick and get him out of here?

There were three pieces, but he was missing one. As he got up and looked around for it, he saw something move by him out of the corner of his eye. He stared long and hard at the tiny little thing on the wall before he moved toward it. It looked like a person, but that couldn't be right either. When he was no more than a foot from it, he saw it blink. Carl fell back on his ass and onto his hands. The pain was only secondary to what he was looking at. It was a tiny little fucking person.

"What the fuck did they put in my lunch?" The thing only stared at him as it hung to the wall. "What are you?"

"Faerie." The voice was just what he'd think a faerie would sound like. Small, almost tinny sounding. "You've been a very nasty person."

"Yeah? So the fuck what? It's not like you can do anything about it." It said that it could if it wished to. "How do you figure that's going to work? You going to come down here and mess me up? I'm thinking that you'd stand a better chance of taking on a leaf than me."

"I am not without friends." Carl snorted, then looked around. This would be the perfect thing to happen to him, he thought. Him sitting on his ass talking to a fucking wall. "You do not believe me? I have many friends that think you should be dead anyway."

"I don't think so. I did nothing wrong. Not so that anyone would be able to catch me, that is." It said nothing but didn't move either. "Why don't you come down here and unlock this door for me? That way you can take me to your many friends and we can see who is the better fighter."

"I never said that I would fight you, moron. I only said that I had many friends. You are the one that inferred that I would cause you harm. And had I wanted to, I would have already."

Carl decided that this was just stupid. Or he was. Getting up, he sat back down on his cot and tried to put the note back together. When the little creature flew by him again, the note mended itself and looked to have never been torn up in the first place. Carl picked it up without a word.

"Carl, I've decided to tell the judge everything I know. That way when you're gone to prison, which you will, I can raise our sons. I swear to you they'll be better off with me than in some fucking home." He looked at the little bug—he decided that was what it was—and snorted again. "Like she knows anything I don't tell her to know."

But he worried now. He wondered first of all how she'd gotten Barney to bring him the note, and secondly, what did she think she was doing leaving him here to rot in prison? Did she not realize that he was the head of the household and that he ruled things? Seriously? She didn't really think that she was going to simply be their leader, did she? Fucking bitch. Not to mention, what sort of lawyer would she even know? The only socializing that they ever did was to promote himself and the boys. She wouldn't even go to parent teacher conferences for fear of making a mistake that would make them all look poorly. His wife, in a word, was a slug. And a lazy one at that. Carl looked at the bug again.

"Oh, she kept herself looking good, even after having the boys for me. But she was never up to par with the women that I fucked. Her affairs, and there were a lot of them, were more of the one fuck thing rather than any kind of fun. She had an itch, and whoever it was scratched it for her." Bug said nothing. But it did go to the window and sit on the ledge. "There was one time in our marriage that we had this thing we had to attend. I don't remember what it was, but she was such a fucking moron at it. One of the ladies asked her what she did all day, and she actually told her that she lay in bed awaiting my return in the event that I wanted a good cuddle. Do I look like the cuddling type to you?"

"Nay, you look like someone that could easily strangle someone that was too close to you. Much as you did with young Beth. You know that poor girl's family still looks for her to return to them? They are without closure." Carl looked around to see who had heard Bug talking. "My name is not Bug. I'm Dark Bloom. And I'm a female, not a thing."

144

"Same thing, if you ask me. But really? Your name is Dark Bloom? What were your parents on when they gave you that name?" She told him she had no parents. "Not even possible there, little girl. Everyone has parents. Even a shit ball like me has them."

"The faerie queen created us. There is no parent in it, but we do have sisters and brothers a plenty. I was born in the year of the great spring. There were tens of thousands of us created that year." Like Carl was going to believe that. Instead he looked down at the note again. "I would guess that a man such as yourself would not believe in magic either. That's too bad. It is all around you, all the time. I believe your wife believes."

"That's because she's stupid. And if she thinks she's going to tell me what she's going to do, I have news for her. She is mine, and I'll tell her when she can make a fucking decision." Carl eyed the bug...err, faerie. "Can you take her a note for me? I don't know what you're doing here, but you can do that for me, can't you? I'll pay you well for it."

"I have no use for money, and neither do you right now. As for taking your mate a note, I won't do that either. She will be going to prison with you, but because you have made her a doormat all her life, she'll never survive. She's no longer a bastard like you are." There was a tone there he was sure, but Carl chose to ignore it. "Your sons, would you like to know about them?"

"Billy is going to be just like his old man. Carter is not like any of us. I swear, there are times when I think he was switched at birth and I was given a girl instead of a son. I'm thinking he'll go on to be some pussy whipped man that his wife rules. She'll even carry his balls in a plastic bag in her purse." Dark Bloom only shook her head. "You know this for a fact, or are you going to be telling me some more lies?"

"I do not lie. We cannot." Sure, Carl thought. Everyone lies about something. "Billy will be dead before the end of the week. He will try to rob a store for cash and will be shot in the chest once. He will suffer badly for it, but in the end, he too will die. He does not care for being without, and felt, as I have discovered you do, that if he wishes to have it, then it will be his."

"No, not Billy. Mother fuck, you'd better be lying." She told him again that she couldn't lie. "What can I do to make it so he doesn't get killed? Where is his brother in all this? Standing beside him no doubt, watching the whole thing go down."

"Nay, Carter is at his foster home. Feeling secure for the first time in his life. He might, however, die before he turns eighteen if there is no one to intercede on his behalf. He is in the wrong place at the wrong time, and is killed when the home that he's in is robbed at random. But I think, should things go differently for him, and someone comes to help him, he will live a good long life." Dark smiled at him. "You, however, might go on to live longer than anyone wishes. I think it sad that you would outlive most of the people that you hurt. There are a great many people who will take exception to the way you speak to them as well. If you make it to prison, you are gang raped by at least a dozen inmates, as well as stabbed in the men's room at the prison. Many will be there when it occurs, but sadly no one sees it. Your death goes unsolved. And this should be no surprise to you, no one really cares enough to look into it."

"Shut up." She said nothing, but she did laugh. "You think this is funny? Why are you even here? What the fuck can you possibly want with being here with me? Money? I have plenty of it, but you said you have no use for it. Fame? Honey, just showing yourself to someone would give you all the fame you want. What do you want?"

"I have been asked to come here and watch over you. And if the opportunity comes up, I'm to steer you in the right direction that will expedite your death. That's not really what I was told...I was told to not help you should the time come when you are being murdered. As I have said, you are not a nice person." He asked about his wife. "Her watcher is to do the same. It has come to our attention that your wife, unbeknownst to you, obviously, is quite the murderess too. Did you know that she is responsible for the death of your first wife? As well as your mother and father? Well played, if you ask me. And now, if she gets off by turning you in, she will get the stashes of money that you told her about in the event you were ever in a position that you could no longer come home. Sad really, when you think her as stupid as she does you."

Carl sat down. It was not true. There was no way any of this was true. But the longer he sat there thinking, the more he could see enough truth in it to make him want to find his wife and murder her with her own guts. Mother fuck, Carl thought, he'd been had.

And his sons? They were both to die? That could not be possible. They were just kids, his kids. He'd taught them to run when things got hinky. And if they were in a situation where there didn't seem to be a way out, to shut the fuck up and call an attorney. He needed to get to Billy. The boy would need to be safe. Carl sat, trying to figure out how to get him some money so he'd be flush again. Poor boy, to be without his things must be hurting him. But no matter how much he tried to think about it, he just couldn't make it work. The fucking Bentleys were going to pay. This was entirely their fault.

Chapter 11

Pip woke and found herself alone in the big bed. But she could hear the shower running and decided to go and see what Burke was doing up so early. Or perhaps he was just getting home. A patient had called to say that she was in labor, and he'd left about eleven last night to see if he could bring another babe into the world. His favorite part of his job, he'd told her.

Not even bothering with the sheet to wrap around her, she walked into the bathroom to find that not only was he leaning against the wall with the water streaming over him, but he appeared to be asleep. Dropping to her knees in front of him, she touched her tongue to his cock.

Pip watched as his cock thickened and stretched. Taking just the crown into her mouth, she swirled her tongue around the curve of him and then sucked on him enough to have him moan. Cupping his balls in her hand, she took him deeper into her mouth past the tightness of her throat and swallowed. She looked up at him when he touched the back of her head to bring her closer to him.

"Yes." His body was beautiful, hard in all the right places, seemingly sculpted from a hard stone. He was straining now that he was fully awake, and she loved it. "Don't stop. Suck on my cock until I come. Then I'll think of some way to repay you." She let go of his cock and licked him from root to tip again before speaking.

"You want to fuck me bent over the counter?" He nodded. "I'd like that. Very much. And then when we're done, you can eat me."

"How about if you suck my cock, then I place you on the counter and eat you before I fuck you?" Pip told him that sounded perfect. "Take me, Piper. I want to come so badly now."

His cock was almost too thick for her mouth now. Fisting him while she bobbed up and down over his length, she moaned when he cupped the back of her head again and held her to him while he pounded her. Sliding her hand down her belly to her pussy, she slid her fingers into her heat and played gently with her clit while she thought of all the things Burke was going to do to her when it was his turn.

When he pulled her back, his fist wrapped tightly around his cock, she watched as he let go. Each stroke of his fist brought more and more of his cream to her body, and she caught some of it in her open mouth. Tasting him this way, feeling his cum burn into her skin and mouth, she nearly came when he told her to clean him. Taking him back in her mouth, she fucked him with her mouth until he pulled her away again.

"Too much. It's too much." He pulled her from the floor and turned off the water almost in the same movement. Taking her out of the stall, he tossed her up onto the counter and his cat took him before she could tell him what she wanted. As soon as his nubby tongue touched her clit, Pip came, screaming out his name. Pip loved the big animal as much as she did his counterpart. The two of them were hers.

His big cat fucked her hard with his tongue, making her come over and over until she was weak with it. Then Burke was there. Watching him, his transformation not quite complete, she wondered if the panther was holding him, as if he wanted to be there when Burke fucked her. Then he was gone and Burke was talking to her.

"Lean back." She did as he commanded and lay back on the counter. It wasn't nearly long enough, but he turned her enough that she could lay over the counter and he could stand between her legs. "When you come, I'm going to take your throat. Mark you again until I'm satisfied you no longer smell like my brothers."

"They said it would drive you insane. Every time one of them would hug me, they'd tell me they were making your cat jealous." He slammed deep, his body powering into her as he held her legs up to his shoulders. "Burke, please, I need to come too. Hurry, I need to come. Release in me, now, Burke."

He held her this way, making it nearly impossible for her to come. Her clit was on fire, and her breasts hurt to be suckled. When he let her legs go finally and pinched her clit, Piper came hard enough to feel it to her very core. Then he leaned over her and kissed her savagely.

"Now you have to come for me." She shook her head and he growled. "Come for us so that we can mark you as ours."

"No, we have to mark each other again. I need to taste you as well." She could see his cat again, his black fur eating at Burke until it was hard to tell which was fucking her. "I want to mark you. Sink my fangs into your throat and taste your blood."

She thought he'd argue, or at the very least tell her no. But he tilted his head in a way that had her hungering for him. Not just his blood, but all of him. And when he came, throwing back his head and howling like only a cat could, Pip pulled his wrist to her mouth and bit down.

He nearly knocked her to the floor, his thrusts became so violent. And when he came again, this time taking her throat, Pip cried out, screaming his name as he drank greedily from her wound. Coming again, feeling the darkness of exhaustion nearly take her under, she held onto Burke and knew that she'd be safe. She succumbed to it just as he dropped atop her.

When she woke the next time, Pip knew she was alone in the bedroom. Stretching out on the cool sheets, she found the note that Burke had left on his pillow.

"Anytime, and I do mean anytime, you ever want to join me in the shower like that, you come on ahead. Christ, I think you hurt me in a few places." She giggled. "But on a serious note. Shane is awake. They have run a lot of tests, and he seems to not have any ill effects of the attempt on his life. The doctor said that in a few days they'll get him up, but it looks good."

She was so happy that she got up and danced around the room before heading into the bathroom to take a shower. She had things to do today...a meeting with Howie, as well as a few things she needed to get going in the greenhouse. It was going to be a wonderful day, she thought.

Pip was scrubbing her hair when she realized what she'd been thinking. A wonderful day was not something that she would have thought possible, not even a few weeks ago. And now here she was not just happy, but feeling like she had everything that she could have ever hoped for. And she refused to wonder when the other shoe was going to drop.

As she was trying to decide what to wear to a business meeting with Howie, she felt the faint touch of someone at her mind. They weren't good at it—lack of practice, she thought—but when she realized who it was, she sat down on the bed and waited.

I wasn't sure this was going to work. It's Shane. I wanted to talk to you. She told him that she'd only just heard that he was awake. Pip asked him how he was feeling. *Good. I'm sore and hurt a lot, but I wanted to talk to you before they give me more drugs. They make me feel better, but I can't think very well. I wanted to thank you.*

I should have known you were hurt as badly as you were. You have no reason to thank me. Had it not been for the queen, you'd have passed. He laughed. *I don't think that's funny, Shane. You could have died.*

Yes, and Mom said that you could have too. Along with Walter. You saved us both by coming to us. Neither my mom nor any of the others could have been there in time to do anything. You were, and you saved us both. She said nothing. *Those men, you took care of them too, didn't you? So that they'd not hurt anyone, especially me again. I remember you saying something about that, something about a car, but not much else. It's fuzzy, what happened that day. But I do know that you were there when no one else could be.*

They had to die for hurting my family. I hated to use that poor man, but your father, he made it right for him. He has a new car and some money for his trouble. Shane told her that he loved her. *And I you, Shane. Both you and Walter. I wish I had known you were injured as badly —*

Am I dead? She wasn't sure what he was asking her and asked him what he meant. *I'm only here, all of us are here and happy, because of you. Had you not done anything, as you told me most people wouldn't, there would be a great deal of sadness for my family. The best outcome I can think of is what you did. Did you do what you could to save us both? Did you give up nearly all of your magic to keep us from dying? Don't answer that. I know you did. Not only did Mom tell me, but everyone has. And for that, you are my hero, now and forever.* She told him there wasn't any way she was his hero. *I can call anyone I want my hero, Pip. And you're mine. You told me that you could come to me quickly. You said that you could take me away. Well, you did one better. You saved my brother and me from being dead. And to me, that's what a hero is.*

Thank you. So very much. I don't think I've ever been anyone's hero before. He told her that he was glad to be the first. *I can feel your pain. You should take your medication and rest. I'll be in later to see you.*

I have one more thing I wanted to tell you. Well, ask you. Great-Grandda and I go fishing every other Saturday when the weather is nice and warm. He says it like that, but we really go every day we can in the summer. I was wondering if you'd see your way to making him a nice place to dig up worms. I know that it's dumb, but he complains all the time about buying them. And when I woke last night, he started telling me about all the fishing we were going to do, him and me. Pip wiped the tears off her face and told him it was a great idea. *He's the best at listening to people by never shutting up. I mean, have you ever heard a man go on about everything like he does?*

He talked to me. Howie is a great man. You could learn a lot from a man such as him. Shane said he knew; he'd told him, but not about what. *I love the old man too. I think he is the glue that holds this family together. Even if they don't want him to.*

I think you're right. He was quiet, and she knew he was talking to someone. *They want to dope me up again. I'm hurting pretty badly, and I want to be okay when you get here later. I can't have any food, but I'm counting on you to sneak me in something special when I can. All right?*

Deal.

She stayed in his mind until he slipped away on the drugs. While she was there, she took a look around his mind, making sure that he wasn't hurting anywhere that might be of a concern. All she found were wounds that were mending well and that he was happy. Shane was going to be just fine. And so was she, Pip thought to herself.

~~~

Katie walked around the big building and could almost see all the things in the nursery that Pip had talked about to them. Howie had brought her along with the promise of lunch afterwards, and she was glad now that she'd taken him up on it. The hour that he'd said it would take had long since passed, and she'd already dug into her stash of granola bars that she kept in her purse. But this was just too much fun to stop now. She looked again at the small items that she knew were going to be a big hit. Handmade items that little faeries had made for their own homes.

"What are you thinking there, love of my life?" She looked up at her mate and smiled. "Oh, I know that look. You had that look when you told me that I should invest in that pants company all those years ago."

"And it paid off well, did it not?" He nodded and hugged her to him. Katie loved this man more than she did her own self. "You think this will work for her and the little people? I mean, it's a big undertaking, even with all our help. I think she has a wonderful head on her shoulders, but she isn't always in a good place. Do you think that will hurt them?"

"Nah. Like you said, she's got a good head on her, and if she needs us, any one of us can come right here and help her. Even our Burke is close enough to come and hold her should she need it. I thought perhaps when I was talking to her about things that you and her had gotten your heads together to bamboozle me about this place. But I can see it now…it'll be a work of art. Little Pip there, she's smart and cautious. Two things that will make it work no matter what. Did you see what she's thinking about the front? And her workers are going to be coming from the shelter. Damned if I don't wish I'd thought of that myself."

"She won't take the building either." He shook his head and Katie knew it was a sore spot for him. He'd wanted to sign the entire place over to her, but she'd refused. "To be honest, I'm not surprised. And her reasons for it are sound. Like she said, what if it doesn't work out? What will she do with a ten thousand square foot building?"

"You think it'll fail?" Katie shook her head and looked over at Pip while she spoke to the two faeries that had come with her. She was sure that they weren't any less cautious than she was. They wanted this to work too much to be taking big chances at the beginning of the game.

"She sure did like the name you thought of. That little feller, Haston, he sure did take a shine to you too." She wondered if Howie was jealous, but thought that was just silly. "I think I'd like to get her a big sign for the place. One you can see for miles and miles. Yes siree, this place is gonna bring them in. People will come just to see the pretties she has here."

"I think you should let her decide on the size of the sign she wants, but I agree. It's going to be a great success. And you should also know that she won't be as easy to wrap around your finger as you think she will be." Howie just snorted at her. "You are not as charming as you might think you are."

"Of course I am. Got you to come and be my mate, didn't I?"

Katie just shook her head. The man was a flirt and a pain in her bottom, but she'd not trade him for all the money in the world. When Pip came toward them, she could tell that the faeries had agreed to their terms.

"Okay, Jibar, you didn't meet him, but he wants to have say over the signage. Not the name of the place, which he loves, but the faerie that is on it. He said that if someone put one of them Tinker women on it, he's not going to help work the place." Howie looked at her, and Katie nodded her agreement. "Good. And there is something else that they want too. It's sort of tricky. They want to be able to put a little magic around and inside the place, so that when someone comes in, they're in a better mood. Not in a mood to buy, but just simply feeling better about life in general."

"They can do that?" Pip nodded and looked back at the little people, as she'd been calling them, before saying they could do a great many things. "I love the idea. I think it would work for the people that will be helping out as well. Yes, what a wonderful idea. What else?"

"Just the few things that we talked about. The plants and flowers will be for sale, but not at out of this world pricing. The larger items, and I'm not really sure what they think those will be, those will be priced accordingly. Again, not sure what that means, but they've sent out some scouts to see about what other shops are asking for things. And getting some ideas too. But they are thinking that when they find them, then they can have some say in the prices. And, of course, the back rooms, the ones where they're going to be working, are off limits to everyone but children. They don't think that they'll tell anyone what they're doing, and we love children."

"I do as well." Howie wiggled his brows at Pip and Katie smacked him on the arm. The man was going to get her all upset, and they were having such a lovely time. "When do you want to start? I'm assuming you want to be open by spring if not before?"

"They can have it open before Christmas if you let them." Katie looked around. The place was in bad shape, not to mention dirty. There had to be an inch of dust on every flat surface in the place. The building had been closed up for some time even before they bought it. Katie looked at Pip when she cleared her throat. "They won't be using conventional means to get it ready. There are a lot of them, and a project like this, it won't take them long to get it done when they set their mind to it. Faeries are very organized."

"Oh yes, of course. Yes. Magic and all that. I think that's a grand idea. Will they...well, of course they decorate for the holidays." Pip nodded and smiled. "I can't wait to see it. I'm getting very excited for this. Aren't you, dear?"

"I'm terrified, if you want to know the truth of it. This is a lot of building, and there are a lot of things that can go wrong when you consider that thousands of different ideas will be put around here before the doors open. Then there are the plants and such. What if no one buys them? And Reggie was telling me that we need to have displays. I was thinking plants on the floor to start with, but apparently that's not the way we are going to do this either. She's been looking for large pieces in the other buildings to put in here to use. Did you know that the water is going to have to be—?" Katie put her hand over Pip's mouth and she grinned. "I'm slightly overwhelmed. I had hoped that you'd say no when we got here. I'm not sure why I thought this would work, any of it to be honest. I don't want it to fail, but I'm worried all the same."

"It will do very well, my child, simply because you're a Bentley." Pip told her that a name was not the cure-all for everything. "Oh, how you doubt me. Wait, you'll see soon enough."

There were some noises in the back of the building and Katie started to go investigate. "Don't, not just yet anyway. You can't move from where we are. They're ready." Katie asked for what. "For you to approve. If the two of you will just say yes, then they're going to get started."

"Now? This very moment?" Pip explained that they, too, were excited. She looked at Howie and he nodded. "Yes, we agree to the terms."

Katie had no idea what she had expected. Yes, some magic, she supposed, but nothing could have prepared her for the way that they did it. A line of the most colorful and brightly lit beings lined up against the wall furthest away from them, and as one they moved. It was like watching a television movie being turned from an old black and white picture to one of the most brilliant of color.

The wall they were against seemed to come alive with movement. As they made their way down it, the dirt just seemed to disappear and colors appeared in the concrete that had been used. The grains of the wood popped out when it was cleaned, the color of it a beautiful contrast to the faeries around it. The metal pipes were brought to their original color. The floor, when they moved down to it, became a shining testament to bygone years when hardwood floors were used, and not the usual concrete.

The counter at the back of the room was emptied of the reams of dusty paper. The stoneware top glistened with a newness it hadn't seen in decades. A cash register appeared from somewhere, its age in perfect harmony with the work that was being brought to life. Katie watched it all.

The windows gleamed when a crew set to work on them.

The sills had been thick with dust and broken glass. Now they were pristine, the windows seamless in their beauty. She'd not even realized that the tops of each of them had stained glass designs, each of them depicting an animal at play with small children.

The front of the building had been boarded up, the large pieces of wood making the room dark without the sunlight. The large glass doors—magic had been used to replace them— had stained glass within their wooden confines as well. This time it was faeries at play, the flowers all around them as bright and lovely as the men and women that worked on it.

As the faeries got closer to them, Pip told them to remain still so that no harm would come to them. The faeries would never cause them harm, but they were set on a task and might inadvertently hurt them if they were in the way. As the little people fluttered and cleaned around them, Katie felt like she was given a rare treat to see them working so hard. The way they made the old building just come to life was an amazing sight to behold, and she would never look at this place the same way again. When they moved beyond them to the rest of the room, Katie turned to Pip and hugged her tightly.

"Oh my, I will never forget this so long as I live. Never." Pip told her that they were a sight to behold. "Yes. I can't wait to see the rest of the building finished now. With the flowers and the big vases. Pip, this is going to be such a success. I can see it now. I could see it before too, but with this...well, people are going to be lining up out the door just to see this place."

"Would you like to see the work area?" Katie nodded and she and Howie followed her to the back. "They're going to sleep here too at times. Especially when the blooms are ready to open. They want to be here to welcome the new ones to this world and take them to where they can grow should they need to. That way the flowers will have a double purpose…to bring more of our kind into the world, as well as to brighten the world a little more."

The transformation, like that in the front room, was amazing. Not just clean, but beautifully decorated with flowers and trees painted on the wall. At the bottom of the largest mural were pots of plants, flowers in full bloom, and roses that trailed up the long pipe and over the ceiling above. Katie felt transported to a land of happiness, the place where faerie tales and color had been created.

"I could live here." Pip smiled at her. "I'm serious. This is beautiful. Oh, how lovely this would be painted on a child's wall. Our granddaughters would love waking up to this every morning. I would love it as well."

"They like color and scents. The plants are from our greenhouse. There are seedlings too that they brought in. We'll plant them in the front pots when the weather is warmer, let them overflow with color. For now, they're going to work on holiday things, wreaths made of heather and bay leaves. I think one of the workers has an idea to decorate a tree, with not ornaments but things from nature. I don't know if anyone will care, but they want to do this. This is…I think of this as their project, not mine." Katie moved over to the table that had been set up. There were boxes and boxes of cookies of every brand and variety. "They'll need the sugar when they're finished. There's juice in the fridge too."

"I could have them some baked." Katie turned to Pip. "These can't be as good for them as ones made at home. And I would love to help out. And juice too. Howie and I could make sure that they have fresh, not the kind that has so many chemicals in it that they'd be ill from it."

"They like cookies made with herbs. Lavender cookies.

Pine nut ones as well." Katie was nodding, her mind going a mile a minute on things they could find for them. "You're going to do this, aren't you? Help them?"

"Yes. Oh yes. And I'll love every minute of it if you let me have a discount." Pip told her that they could arrange that. "I'm so happy for you and your friends, Pip. This is going to be so successful. I know I keep saying that to you, but it's true. A faerie garden run by faeries. I swear I would not have believed it had I not seen it with my own two eyes. You're going to have people lined up out the door."

"Not me." Katie had forgotten about that. Pip was going to be more of a behind the scenes sort of business owner. "Reggie and Chris are doing the interviews for workers. Rylee is doing background checks on the ones that they decide they might hire. And the faeries will be here all the time to keep an eye on everyone. The humans won't be able to see them, but the others will. We need people here that can be trusted with that. I think they're going to have so much fun at this. Provided they can keep busy enough."

"I think you're going to be very busy." Howie winked at her as he continued. "Yessiree bob. I think you're going to be very busy just keeping my mate here happy and supplied with all kinds of things for the yard and house."

As they left the building, the place still being cleaned and decorated, Katie tried to think what it would be like, coming to a place like this to work every day. It would be happy, she thought. And full of energy. She decided to talk it over with Howie, but she was going to come here, work a few hours a week. Just to feel like she was a part of something huge. And there was no doubt in her mind that this was going to be very big.

Chapter 12

Burke read over the chart twice trying to make his mind see what he was reading. He finally had to lean back from the file and close his eyes. The ringing of his phone went unanswered. If it were family, they'd know how to get in touch with him.

There is a reason you have that ringing device on your desk. You do know that, don't you? He smiled when Tony spoke to him through their link. Burke told him he was trying to work out a problem. *Yeah, me too. I think yours will be easier to solve.*

What's up? Tony, in his usual fashion, didn't answer him. *I have this patient that I see at least once a week. There is nothing ever wrong with him, but here he comes to see me. At first I thought it was because he was lonely. It still might be that, but I don't think that's all of it. However, he never says all that much, doesn't take up any of my time more than anyone else, and when he's done, he goes home with the promise of not bothering me again.*

Do you suppose he's trying to get a bead on things so he can come back and rob you blind? Burke told him he doubted it. The man was in his nineties. *Doesn't mean a thing. For all you know, he could be this big time drug dealer that cons unsuspecting doctors all the time, and you're his next hit. Next week, you'll come to work and the place will be empty but for those paper rolls of shit you use on those cold assed tables you have.*

Are you always this cheerful? Tony said he was sorry. Burke laughed. *Don't worry about it. Really, what is it? You didn't just reach out because you wanted to bust my chops about the phone.*

I need a favor. Not a big one, but help all the same. I want to buy a home. Not like you have, but a nice sized one. With some land. I'm thinking about becoming a true country vet. Burke asked him what that meant. *Not sure at the moment, but I know that I need to get out of the apartment I'm in and into something that I can call my own. My neighbors are driving me insane. And I'm not happy with being in an office all day long either. I need to...I'm going to buy me one of those big vans and become a traveling doctor. I think I could make it work better than the office I'm using right now.*

You're already nearly completely insane, buddy. Sorry to burst your bubble. Tony told him to fuck off. *Yeah, no need for that, I have a mate. But what is it you want me to do? Look for you? I mean, you can hire someone to do that for you.*

Yeah, I know, but I want you and Pip to go and look at them for me. Pretend you're the ones buying the house and not me. He asked him why. *Because the last three days I've had four different realtors show me a house, and anything that they might have on their bodies as well. Both sexes. I want to remain single for a while longer, if you know what I mean.*

Not really. I love having a mate. He knew that his brother hurt, and said nothing about him finding his own. *You could always get yourself laid that way. Keep house hunting until your pecker, as Grandda calls it, just simply falls off.* Tony told him again to fuck off.

Burke was still laughing when he glanced down at the chart. Mr. Rugby was suffering from depression. He had no idea why he thought that was it, but he knew it was. He picked up the chart with fresh eyes and told Tony what he thought.

He comes in when he needs company. All his appointments are done spur of the moment, like he gets to a point that he can't stand it any longer and he comes here. I talk to him, make a couple of jokes, and he goes home. Tony told him that sounded like as good a reason to see him as any. *Don't you see? This place is his lifeline. He's using this excuse of being ill or thinking he has a fever as a way to come here where there are people to keep him from doing something stupid.*

I guess that does sound better than knocking you off for a few drugs. But I'd not rule it out. Tony laughed when he did. *But seriously, you should try and help him find something to do. I don't mean so he stops coming in to see you. He could be like old Craig down at the diner. Did you know that he's still serving coffee for Reggie, as well as ringing out cash?*

He did know that, and the man seemed to be enjoying it too. *Okay, thank you. Now about your house. As a matter of fact, I can help you out with a home. I was looking at two of them when Myra stepped in and set Piper and I up. I'll see what I can find out about them and get back to you.*

Thanks so much. Don't forget, too, that I'm going out of town for a couple of days. I'm going to just catch the last couple of days of the conference. Then I'm flying back. I don't want to go anyway, but I'm speaking on one of the panels. Burke said he'd keep an eye on his place too. *Okay. Oh, the man Elroy Baker, the cook. He's decided to take the building that Grandda showed him. I got an email from him this morning. I have no idea why I got the email instead of Grandda, but if you could tell him, I'd appreciate it.*

I'll tell him today. When do you leave? Tony said he was on his way to the airport now. *Nothing like giving us notice. So will you be home for our Thanksgiving? It's going to be Monday. Then next week is Christmas.*

Yes, I'll be there for both. I'm looking forward to it. It'll be nice to have both Shane and Walter home. Burke agreed. *All right, brother, I'll see you in a few days. Thank you for helping me out.*

After they closed the connection, Burke read over his chart with a better understanding of Mr. Rugby. As Burke made notes on the chart now, he felt better and better. He knew that Mr. Rugby might be hard to convince he needed to get out of his house more, but he'd put Piper on it. Perhaps he could work at the new nursery. Faerie Tales and Dreams was going to open in a couple of days, and maybe they needed someone to hand out flyers at the door or something. Anything to get the man some much needed interaction.

Burke saw two more patients before he was ready for lunch. He'd been thinking about going down to the diner, and was picking up his coat to do that when he saw his mom in the lobby of their offices. Nolan was there as well, and they invited him to come along with them. Burke thought it was a wonderful way to brighten up his day.

"I want to get a job." Burke wasn't sure what to say to his mom when she blurted that out after giving their orders to the waitress. "I don't know how to approach anyone about it, but I'd hoped that you two could give me an idea."

"Who is it you want to work for?" She told him. "I'm pretty sure that Piper will be thrilled to have you come work with her. In fact, all she's talked about since last night is how much fun she had with Grandma and Grandda. What is it you had in mind?"

"I have no idea. I've never had a job before." She laughed nervously. "When your dad was alive, it was easier for me to be a stay at home mom to be there for you boys. There was always enough money, you know, but your dad worked because his dad did. And Katie is going to go in a few hours a week too. She's going to be showing people around that might need help. I want to…I was thinking I could help put the displays together. You know, tote some of the bigger things out to the floor for the little people."

"Mom, I don't think you should be—" Burke kicked Nolan in the shin under the table. "Ouch, what was that for?"

"Mom should be able to do what she wants when she wants. Anything."

Nolan opened his mouth and then looked at their mom. She was glaring at Nolan, and Burke decided he'd leave him to it the next time.

"Thank you, Burke. I always knew you were my favorite son." She looked at Nolan then. "And what is it you think will happen to me, Nolan? Do you suppose that I'm too old? That I might fall and break a hip? Do you think me too feeble minded to do a good job? Tell me, Nolan Patrick Bentley, what is it you don't think I can do?"

"Mom, what I meant was…." Nolan looked at Burke. "Damn it. I didn't mean anything by it. Now I'm looking bad because of you."

"Watch your language, young man." Nolan dropped his head. "Burke didn't get you into trouble. He was trying to save you. But I am going to work. And I am going to have fun at it. The nerve of you thinking that…. I think I'm going to tell Rylee on you."

"*No!* Please, God no. I'm so sorry, Mom. Really I am. I just worry about you, not because of your age or thinking that you can't do it, but.... Well, to be honest with you, I hate that you feel you need to get a job. I had hoped that we'd provided for you better than that." She looked angered a bit, then smiled. "I love you, as we all do, and we want you happy."

"Good save, and I am happy. And I don't need the money. But I do need to feel useful. When the babies are bigger and need to be sat once in a while I'll be all over that, but I don't like just sitting around the house with nothing to do." She huffed at him then. "And I will not be joining any women's or book clubs. Or any other such nonsense. I love to read, but I think sitting around with other people talking about it is just boring."

"You should do it then." She nodded and winked at him when Nolan approved. "I don't mean that to sound like you needed my permission to do it. But I can worry. You're my mom, after all."

"I am. But I'm also alive. I need this." Burke talked to Piper about it and she told him to tell his mom if she came over to the shop right now, she'd put her to work.

Is something wrong? Want me to come over too? She said she wasn't sure and he felt her depression hit him in the heart. *Piper, what is it?*

I'm having a meltdown.

Burke stood up and told them he was leaving. Even before he was to the door, his mom was with him. Nolan, she told him, was taking care of the check. As they hurried across the street and down a few blocks, all he could think about was getting to her. Had his mom not been with him, he would have stepped in front of a car, he was so worried about Piper.

She was in the back room curled into a tight ball on the floor. The faeries were all around her, and he could see that they were upset as well. Kneeling in front of her, he took her hands into his and held them. When she sobbed that she was hurting, Burke picked her up in his arms and held her. Burke saw his mom go out into the front of the shop, and he could hear her talking to someone.

"We were putting together that stupid tree over there." He glanced at the empty box and the branches of a Christmas tree spread all around a tall pole. "Then Jibar comes back to tell me that the flowers that we put in the window need to be watered or they'll die. It just took me under."

He wasn't sure what to say so he just held her. Piper had told him that saying anything wasn't important when she was down, but being there was. There wasn't anything he could do but hold her, and she'd get over it.

Piper cried for another ten minutes, babbling about plants dying and instructions that were in too many languages to be very useful. Still he held her, feeling as useless as he'd ever felt before. When she quieted, he told her about Mr. Rugby and him maybe needing a job.

"I met him." He asked her when. "About three months ago. I'd decided to go to this meeting. Something about dealing with depression. I can't remember what tag they put on it. About halfway through the thing I decided that it was horseshit. I think Mr. Rugby did as well. We left at the same time."

"He's a cantankerous old man. Tells me each time that he comes in that I need to do this or that to my offices." She nodded and leaned back so that she could look up at him. "I love you so very much, Piper. With all that I am."

"I love you too. I'm sorry about this." He kissed her and she smiled at him. "You do make a nice buddy when I get like this. I don't...I think I frightened poor Jibar. He was only making a suggestion and I completely lost it."

"He'll be just fine. I'm betting that the flowers are now watered and that he's making plans to make sure they're well taken care of from now on." Piper snuggled up under his chin and he held her that way as he continued. "My mom is more than likely out there making those poor creatures shake in their boots. She said that she needed to be doing something. Grandma too, did you know that?"

"Your grandma came in early this morning, and has been putting dirt in the big pots in the greenhouse here. She and some of the others have been at it a while, so I'm betting she's had enough." Burke doubted it but said nothing. "Rylee came by after that with a truckload of furniture that she said was in one of the vacant buildings that you all own. I'm pretty sure that she's not telling me all of it. But she had fun, and so did the young boys from your brother's leap. Despite the fact that they're terrified of her, they managed to laugh a bit. I ordered them sandwiches from the diner when they wouldn't take any money for helping me out."

"To be honest with you, I'm afraid of all my sisters-in-law. And my mom. My mom can make me feel ten years old again and out of my element with just a look." He told Piper about Nolan at lunch. "I tried to stop him, but he was on a roll."

"You should use that threat again sometime. Nolan loves his wife very much, but like you, he's afraid of her." He asked if she was. "No, not really. She does tend to intimidate me a little, but I'm getting better at blowing her off. Your grandma scares me. She's a sneaky kind of scary. You think she's all fluff and fun, but I'd not want to be on her bad side. She could tear you apart in a heartbeat."

After a few minutes she got up. Watching her and still feeling her sadness, he wondered if she'd be all right or would like to go home. But she told him she was going to get this tree done and he needed to go back to work. Standing, he felt like he needed to stay.

"If you do then I'm going to get nothing done today." He nodded. "Will you have Mr. Rugby come and see me? I think I have a job for him during the grand opening next week. And if he wants, he can stay on as a worker for us."

Burke helped her with the tree. To be honest, the sucker was difficult to put together, but they got it, with only one branch left over. Then he helped her move it to the showroom floor. It was time he got back to work anyway.

On the way back he decided that coming to work with his brother was the best thing that could have happened for him. He could come and go as he needed, just like today. He was closer to his family because he wasn't working all the time, and if he wanted, he could find his mate, chase her in the woods, go flying with her, or anything else he wanted because he was no longer exhausted. Burke was a happy man.

~~~

Carl was lying on his cot, contemplating all the things he was going to do when he got out of here. And even though his attorney told him that they'd found two of the women's bodies that Roach had put references about in his little books, he knew nothing was going to stick. He had a plan too. And it ended with him being a free man with all his money.

"Mr. Mason." He didn't bother looking up at the sound of the voice any more. He'd been trying to get them to let him go for five days now, or at least let him see his sons, but he was denied. "Mr. Mason, you have a visitor."

"I don't want to see anyone that isn't in my living room at my own home." The person laughed. "You think this is funny now, but you wait until I'm free of here. You shits are going to pay for my treatment."

"And how do you think the people that you murdered feel about the treatment you had of them?" He knew that voice. Carl looked at Nolan Bentley and snarled at him. "Tisk, tisk. Is that any way to treat a visitor? I'm sorry that it's not in your living room. But you no longer have one anyway, so it's doubtful that you'd entertain there any time in the future."

"What do you mean, I don't have a living room? I most certainly do." Nolan unfolded the chair Carl had only just noticed. "Don't get comfy, Bentley. I have nothing to say to you."

"Oh, well that's too fucking bad. I have a great deal to say to you." He opened his briefcase and took out a file. "My sons are doing much better, in the event you were going to ask. Walter is going to have to wait until spring to go back to college, and Shane is going to need a little more care at home as well. Your sons, I've heard, aren't faring well at all."

"Carter is a pussy. Billy? I heard he's having a rough time of it, but he's a Mason. He'll come around." Bentley said nothing but stared at him. Carl thought he looked a little uncomfortable. "What is it you came here to tell me? What the fuck is it now?"

"I'm sorry. I was told that...I guess he did say that he'd told Mrs. Mason. I assumed.... Well, I'm sorry to tell you, but Billy is in the hospital. He was shot the day before yesterday trying to rob an off-duty police officer in a grocery store. I thought you knew." Carl shook his head and sat up. "Your son was armed. They're still trying to figure out where he'd gotten the gun, but when he tried to use it on the officer, he fired back. Billy was shot once in the chest."

"You're lying. I don't know why you'd think it was funny to say such a thing to me, but you're lying." Bentley said that he wasn't. "Fuck you. Just fuck you. Tell me where he is. And my wife. Tell her to come here and tell me to my face."

"I'm sorry, Carl, but she's not going to be able to come here either. You know that." Carl got up and shook the bars on his cell, screaming for someone to come and tell him where his son was. Bentley said nothing, but only sat in his chair as he watched him. Carl didn't fucking care. He wanted to know about his son.

"What the heck are you doing now?" Barney. It was him again. "Get back from those bars and I'll talk to you. You're gonna have to—"

"My son. Where is he? This fuck told me that he's in the hospital with a gunshot wound to the chest. I want you to tell him he's a liar." Barney looked at Bentley, then back at him, and Carl knew Bentley was telling the truth. His knees simply gave out and he slipped to the floor. "No. No. No. Not my son. Not my baby boy."

Carl couldn't contain his pain. His son was hurting in the hospital and these jackasses were keeping him from him. He looked at Bentley and felt his anger toward the man and his family take him.

"You motherfucker. This is all your fault. I want you to tell them to let me out of here so I can go to my son. He needs his father." Bentley said nothing, didn't even move. "You hear me? I said to get up and tell them to let me go. My son is in the hospital. Doesn't that mean shit to you?"

"You mean like you put my sons there? When you sent out those men to take them out, you mean like that?" Bentley stood up then, and Carl thought he was going to leave him here without helping him. "You can rot in there for all I care. I'm sorry about your son, I am. But you did this to them by trying to kill my boys."

"I never meant for him to try and kill them both. Just that little one. The one that thought he was better than my boys. And so far as I'm concerned, the world would have been a better place without them here. You're just lucky that he didn't get to come after you and that fucking wife of yours when I told him to." Carl opened his mouth to tell him more, to rub it in his face how he'd done this or that, when he realized what he'd said already. "You did this. You lied to me to get me to say things that weren't right."

"I did nothing of the kind." When he started for the door, Carl called him back. All Bentley did was flip him off by lifting his hand up over his head as he continued to move toward the door. Barney stood there staring at him.

"You have just shit in the fan and got it all over you, didn't you?" Carl wanted to ask him what he'd heard, or what he thought he heard, when he spoke again. "Your son is really in the hospital. I tried to tell you the first day when I brought you your dinner, but you told me not to speak to you again. I wanted to even after that, but you cut me off. It's all been recorded too. Just like this here last conversation."

"I wasn't in my right mind. I was grief stricken." Barney only shook his head and turned to leave him too. "Tell them I want to see my boy. There is no reason for me to be in here when he needs me."

He didn't stop either. The only thing that was different in their leaving him was that Barney didn't flip him off. But the finality of their departure was heartbreaking to him. They were doing nothing to let him see his little boy.

"I told you what was going to happen." He turned to look at the bug that had been relentless in her pursuit to drive him insane. "I'm not driving you anywhere, Carl. You're well on your way to doing that all on your own. And now you've just confessed to the attempted murder of Nolan's sons. That is not going to go well for you, I'm afraid."

"He made me do it." She only stared at him. "You heard him, he was taunting me. Saying things that just aren't true. I

Burke

said that back to him because...he pissed me off."

"Did he? I just assumed that you are in a constant state of pissed off." She moved to stand on the bar just out of his reach. "You should know that your son, Billy, he does not make it. I'm sorry for that, truly I am."

"No. Please, you have to help him. He's just a kid." She pointed out that so were Nolan's sons. "I don't give a shit about Bentley's kids. They were in the way and I needed them gone. What would have happened when the boys had some fun with that girl? Nothing. She would have cost us a little bit of money. So? It's not like there isn't plenty more where that came from. And they both would have been with a woman. Every boy should have their first fuck with someone that can't tell them what they're doing wrong. It would have been perfect but for the nosey kid."

"You condone this? This practice of raping a woman when she isn't able to fight back?" He said that it wasn't rape. "How do you think that is possible? Wouldn't he have taken her against her will?"

"You're twisting things all up to suit yourself. She was going to a party were there were boys. What did she think was going to happen? Women who cry rape should really be shown what rape is. Then they'll shut their mouths." He looked up at the camera and wondered if anyone in this stupid station knew how to run it. "Carter and Billy were just going to have a little fun with her. And if she called us on it, then we would have paid her off. It's the way things are done."

"No, they are not." He watched her flitter about in the long hall. He started to go back to his bed to try and think. He needed to see his boy. Wanted to make sure that he was getting the best of care. These idiots were going to pay if he did indeed die. His son was a Mason, after all. "You are a horrible man,

Carl Mason. And I think I will be happy to be done with you. You are not fit to be called human."

When she disappeared, he stuck his tongue out at her. Then at the camera that he was sure wasn't working. As he laid down, thinking of ways to get them to let him go, he had a thought. They were lying to him about his son. Just to get him to say things, as he had, by messing with his head. Carl wasn't going to speak to any of them again, not even his fucking attorney. If he ever came back. He might have fired him yesterday.

Getting up sometime later, he turned and looked at the door. He stared at it for several minutes, just wondering if what he was seeing was real. The door was open. Wide too. Making his way to it slowly, just waiting for someone to come and tell him to get back, he was nearly down the hall to the door when he had to run back to get his shoes. Carl was almost afraid to go back into his cell, but was in and out quickly. He was nearly giddy with happiness as he made his way to the door again.

"Stop where you are." Carl looked at Barney. "What the hell are you doing out of your cell? Get back in there. Now."

Barney pulled his gun and Carl took off running. They were not going to keep him back there when his family needed him. As the first shots rang out, Carl started laughing. He was fucking getting out of here.

Chapter 13

Joey wasn't sure how he felt right now. Carl was dead, killed while trying to escape from jail an hour ago. He'd been... well, Nolan and David had been the last two people to talk to him. And he'd confessed to having Nolan's boys nearly killed.

"Son?" He looked over at his grandda. He figured he'd been sitting there a while. His glass was empty of tea and the condensation was gone as well. "Are you okay? You had nothing to do with his decision to run."

"I know that. I just...I don't know what I feel, to be honest with you. Sort of relieved, but again, like justice wasn't served for Shane and Walter." Grandda nodded. "His son passed away too. Nolan just let me know. The police are on their way to the jail now to tell Milly that her son is gone, as is her husband. Her attorney has also been notified."

"I'm guessing that you'll drop the case now." He said that

it was out of his hands now, the state would take it from there. "I see. They're gonna try a dead man. Sounds like something they'd do."

"It's to ensure justice for everyone, Grandda. Not just Shane and Walter, but for the men and women that helped save them. For the man who hit the would-be killers with his car. He will get his money from the estate now. The hospital will sue as well, for the money to care for Nolan's sons. It's the way they can get it from the Mason estate."

"I guess so. Still, it seems sort of sad, don't you think?" Joey thought it did as well. "What happens to that other boy of his? Carter? Do you think he'll turn out all right now that his daddy isn't in his life anymore?"

"His grandmother showed up at the foster home yesterday, and the two of them talked. He wasn't much like his brother or father, I guess. Just a kid caught between two strong forces. She's going to take him back home with her, raise him as he should be. One of the faeries is going with him, just to make sure that he stays on the straight and narrow." He thought of the faerie that had come to see him not an hour ago. "I don't know what I should do with the information that I have now."

Dark Bloom had come to him while he had been working on a schedule for the horses to be taken to their new homes. She'd told him what she'd done and why. The door was easy, she'd told him, and the rest of it had been up to Carl.

"He was not forced to run, my lord. I only opened the door to see if he would or not. I had hoped things would turn out the way that they did, but you cannot know with humans. He was going to be put away, but no justice would have been served by it. His fate was for him to be put in a lovely home for the insane, where he would have escaped and murdered again." He asked her if she knew this for a fact. "Yes, my lord, I did. I had not thought him talking to me would make a good case for him. The attorney that he told about me, he was working on it. The recordings were going to prove that he was indeed a man that did not have all his facilities."

"So you opened the door for him to try and escape on his own." Dark had nodded, then lay down before him, her wings spread out behind her. "What is this? Regret at what you've done?"

"Nay, my lord. I will never regret what I have done to this man. For to me, he deserved much worse than he got." She looked up at him. "I humble myself before you, give myself over to you to do with as you please. Even at the risk of my own death."

"You think I would kill you? For you opening a door to a man who nearly murdered all that I love?" She said it was the least she deserved for helping a man to his death. A human. "No, I don't want you to die. I don't know what I'll do with you, but I don't want you to die. There has been too much death now."

She said that he had to do something. "I will do as you wish within the bounds of my kind. But you should know that there is little that I wouldn't do for you and your family.

"What if I asked you to serve me? To live here helping me with...I don't know, with the horses should they need it. With my mate should she want something. I would like for you to watch over us and show us where we can improve things to be safe for our children."

"I do that now, my lord." Dark looked at him. "If you would wish this, my lord, I will serve you in any way you need me to do."

He wasn't sure what that entailed and asked her if he could decide later. When she nodded and left, he'd had the feeling then, and still did, that having someone named Dark Bloom serve him wasn't going to be all creams and lotions… something he'd heard his grandma say recently. And now he sat, nearly three hours later, and still no idea what he was supposed to do or even to feel.

Grandda asked him what he wanted to do. Joey had not a single clue, idea, or even a thought that would even begin to cover the fucked up shit going on his mind. He looked out the window when he heard the crunch of gravel.

"The horses." Grandda nodded but neither of them moved. "Chris and I are going to bring a baby into this world. What do we do to keep it safe? How did you do it with all of us getting into trouble?"

"You do the best you can. Your momma, she fretted over you guys a great deal. Forever thinking that if any of you got hurt, someone would come and take you from her." Joey remembered his mom being upset when one of them would fall pretty good. "You just do what you can, son. It's the best you can hope for. But you do know that with all the magic that goes around here and the other houses, it's a damned sight harder to knock you off than it ever was when you were boys."

"What about our children? Shane and Walter, they were covered by the same magic. But we nearly lost them." Grandda told him that he didn't lose them. "But we almost did."

"You can almost yourself into an early grave. You almost made a killing on the market. You almost got hit by a car. You almost forgot to turn on the light switch. All of them almosts, they don't mean a hill of beans if they never came to pass. You should be thinking on the things that happened. I found me a good woman to grow old with and have a child. I got me a good family that I love with all my heart. I'm gonna go fishing with my grandsons before I get too old to bait a hook. These are things that I think of all the time. And what's for dessert."

Joey grinned. "Of course you'd think of your next sugar fix. And as for the other, you're never going to be too old for that. I'm sure of it." Grandda thanked him. "I worry. More and more daily."

Grandda stood up and so did he. Joey was out the door before Grandda stopped him again. "You should worry. Not to the point where it's eating you alive, but worry all the same. Them horses out there for example. What do you suppose they worry about being all locked up in that trailer? Whether or not you're gonna kill them? Maybe they want you to, they've been hurting for so long. Or do you think they're thinking on how they're going to hurt one of you if you get yourself too close? More'n likely. I'd say they got more worries than we can even begin to think on. But you go out there, love them, give them what they need, and things turn out just fine, don't they?"

"Most of the time, yes they do." Grandda nodded. "How is it you get smarter every time I see you? Grandma feeding you some sort of brain food?"

"No, sir. I've always been the brilliant one, you're just starting to notice it because I don't let myself hide under a bushel anymore." He started down the stairs to the trailer before turning back to Joey. "You wanna worry about something? Here's a good one. What you gonna get that pretty bride for Christmas that's going to outdo what I got her?"

~~~

Tony leaned back against the seat and closed his eyes. He was going on vacation, just as soon as he.... No, he told himself. He was going to go on a vacation where he didn't have to tell people how not to take care of their own pets. This conference, one that had been almost a total waste of time and money, had opened his eyes to a great many things. And why have it in the sunny state of Florida when no one wanted to go out and enjoy any of it? When someone tapped him on the shoulder, he opened one eye and looked at the little girl sitting next to him.

"My grandma is going to pick me up at the gates." He nodded and closed his eye again. "Then we're going to live in a cardboard box, because my daddy is a skin flat and he won't give her enough support to raise a cat. That's what my aunt said."

"Skin flint. And your aunt sounds like a peach." The little girl told him that she wasn't, not really. "I see. And you've been living with her? Your aunt? Where is she?"

"Home, and yes, I've been staying with her until Daddy gets home. But she said I was too much for one woman to handle. I tried to be good, but I'm too much. My momma was in the army, but she got herself killed. Aunt Carol said she more than likely is hiding out so she don't have to own up to her responsibilities. I think she means me and Daddy." Tony looked over at the little girl who looked incredibly sad and lonely. "My daddy is in the army too. He's alive, but he can't come home yet until his duty is over. Aunt Carol said that his duty is here, but she thinks he's hiding too. She doesn't like them much. She don't like me either, I guess."

"Does your grandma have a house, or is she really living off the streets?" She told him that she had a house just fine, but it didn't have a swing set. "Those can be bought. But you'll have a roof over your head, and that's what's important."

"I guess so. But I've never met my grandma. Aunt Carol said she's been sloshing hash browns for too long and should retire. But now that I'm in the photo, things aren't ever going to be right for her. She said I'm a burden to all of society." The little girl looked at him shrewdly and seemed to find him lacking in something. "You work? And got yourself a house too? I bet you have a big swing set too."

"No, I don't have a house just yet. My family is helping me find one. And your grandma doesn't slosh hash, but is slinging it. Your aunt have anything good to say to anyone, ever?"

She looked thoughtful, then shook her head at him. "No. She hates everybody. Even my dead beater dad. But I don't know how he's that when he's working hard to stay alive for me. He told me that."

Tony sat up and looked around for someone to help him. Not to leave the little girl, no, that wasn't a problem, but to find out what was going on with her. He spotted the stewardess and asked for something to drink for the two of them, and handed the little girl some cash just to touch her hand.

The little girl's name was Amanda Reynolds, and she was five. Her aunt had dropped her off at the airport with instructions to keep out of trouble, then had left her. Amanda had no luggage other than the bag at her feet, and no jacket or coat to warm herself up in when they landed in a much colder state like Ohio. The woman picking her up was Beth, the little girl's grandma. Tony lay back and tried to think what the fuck he was supposed to do now. He reached out to his own mom and told her what was going on.

Reggie and I are in town with the babies. Chris is here as well. We were going to have lunch. You can join us when we pick you up. What size coat does this little one wear, do you think? He had not one clue and told her that. *She'll have a tag in her clothing that she has on.*

Yeah, I'm sure that'll go over nice. A huge man pulling a little girl in his lap to see what her dress size is. Maybe I can just ask her. He did. *She wears a little one and she likes purple, but her aunt said that purple is for floozies. The woman is all heart, I think. Christ, this was a terrible idea.*

Watch it, young man. I can still beat your bottom for cursing. He told her he was very sorry, but he had this child that was going to freeze if they didn't help. *All right. I'll see what I can do from this end. You say her grandmother's name is Beth? I can see if I can find her at the airport. It won't be too hard I guess, not with the girls with me. Maybe she works at one of the restaurants in town and Reggie might know her.*

Thank you. I don't know what this aunt of hers was thinking, saying stuff like that to a little girl about her parents. And Amanda's father is in the army too, not a dead beater like I'd been told. She asked him what sort of aunt this child had. *I'm thinking not the very loving type. She just dropped this child off at the airport and left her there. The stewardess is worried that the woman won't be there to get her.*

She's her grandma. She'll be there for her. He wasn't so sure. The aunt, however she was related to the grandma, might be just as bad. *I'm in the department store now. Oh, Tony, they have a lovely purple one. I'm going to get her a hat and gloves as well.*

Boots too. She has on a pair of sandals that have seen better days. He reached down and unbuckled the right one and saw the size. *These are a size too small, but they say thirteen on them. That seems odd, don't you think?*

Not really, children's sizes run weird. Zero to thirteen, then they start over at one again when they reach about her age. He helped Amanda with the broken zipper on her back pack and saw the worn books and broken crayons. He felt his heart break for her. *Tony, what is it?*

She has three books in her back pack that are older than I am. About a dozen pieces of crayons that are mostly black. Not to mention the backpack is in poor shape, as if it had been picked up at a trash bin somewhere. His mom said she'd pick that up as well. *I'll pay you back for this. Thanks for doing it.*

It's my pleasure. Oh, and Reggie knows her grandma, but I think she's her great grandma. You know her too. Bethany Spencer. She's one of the cooks at the local elementary school. And while she does have a place to live, it has no yard or any playground area for a little girl. Tony looked over at Amanda, who was coloring on her lap. He pulled the tray down for her and she smiled up at him. *Her father has six more months left on this tour, and yes, his wife was killed about six months ago, but they were divorced. Bethany never said why, but she was pretty upset about it. Carol, the aunt, is actually Bethany's sister, Amanda's great aunt.*

How do you know all this? Or is Chris telling you? She told him, laughing. *Ah, so it's true that Grandma, leaning over the fence – or in your case, volunteering at the school – really does show all their pictures off and talk about their children. Am I ever mentioned in your little gossip sessions?"*

Yes. I tell her what an ungrateful child I've raised and that I'm thinking of kicking his bottom out of my life. Tony smiled. *I tell her that I'm happy with all of my children. There are a few that I'd like to be settled, but I know they have to do that in their own time.*

The pain was like a razor across his heart. His mom didn't know, most of his family didn't know, that his mate was dead. He thought about the conversation he'd had with Pip and let that go too. One chance was all a person got when it came to finding their one true love. He told his mom that they'd be landing in about forty minutes.

Amanda never shut up, but she wasn't nearly as annoying as she might have been had he not known about her circumstances. She was lonely and sad. Her mom was gone, her father out of her life at the moment, and she was going to live with someone that she didn't know at all. Her chatter was nothing more than nervousness. Tony even colored with her for a little while. All in all, it was the best flight he'd ever taken.

185

His family was at the gate with Bethany. She looked as stressed as Amanda did, and when they were closer to them all, Amanda pressed her face into his leg. Tony picked her up in his arms and introduced her to everyone.

"You look like your daddy, did Carol tell you that?" Amanda shook her head at her great grandma. "No, she wouldn't be that kind, would she? Well you do. Spitting image of him. A little of your momma too, but you're your daddy's little girl."

"He said he would come home soon. And that we'd be together." Bethany said that was correct. "I'm sorry that I'm going to be a burden to you. I'll try really hard to be good and not eat too much of your hard earned food."

"Honey, I already baked you some cookies, chocolate chip, and you and I are going to order us a pizza for dinner tonight. Then we're going to make a list of things you're going to need and go shopping tomorrow." Bethany handed her a bag that was brightly decorated. "I got you a pretty gift, but these wonderful people got you a coat and things to wear. Your new friend Tony here, he asked his momma to help us out."

The bear in her bag was a huge hit. And the lavender coat, hat, and gloves fit well. The boots were a little big, but her grandma said she'd grow into them. After gathering up the little luggage that Tony had, he took them all to lunch. By the time they were finished eating, Amanda had worn herself out and was napping in the back of her grandma's car.

"Thank you for what you did for her, Tony. You're a good boy." Tony nodded but said nothing. He was slightly embarrassed. "Her daddy will be home this summer. She and I, we're going to get to know one another, and he's gonna live here with us when he gets out. He's mustering out so he can be here for her. And his sister is coming soon too. She's gonna help me out with the little one."

"If you need anything, just let me know. I've grown fond of her." Bethany nodded and looked at the little sleeping girl. "She will be fine here, I think."

"Much better than she would have done with my sister. Carol has her own standards, and she doesn't care all that much for children. Why Amanda's mom left her with her is beyond me. They weren't related other than my grandson being her husband for a time. I think...I'm not sure, but I think it was the money coming to her from them. As soon as I got wind that she was sending me Amanda, I called Sheppard to let him know that he had to change out his money being sent to her."

"She told me some things, things her aunt said to her, that a little girl should not be made to hear. I have the feeling that she's been put down a great deal." Tony would not normally say anything like that to someone, but he'd already seen how good Bethany was going to be for Amanda. "She thinks that her mother is hiding out to not take responsibility for Amanda."

"They sent her body home when she was killed. If she's hiding out, then she's done a great job of it." Tony nodded, already figuring as much. "You're a good man, Tony. And a good friend to Amanda. Thank you so much for what you did for her. And what you had your momma do. I never thought of coats or boots. I never...well, I never dreamed that Carol wouldn't provide for Amanda. I guess I was wrong about a great many things."

"You said that Sheppard's sister is coming to help you. When do you expect her?" Bethany looked at Amanda again. "What is it? I want to help you all."

"Her ex-husband left her in a mess. He was killed a few months ago, and Coleen is trying to close up some things. Micky wasn't a good man, nor was he very smart, but he could get into trouble faster than anyone we knew. When he and Coleen divorced a few years ago, I thought that she'd finished with him. Apparently he dragged her back in after he was gone. Making her responsible for his things as well as a few unpaid bills. She's coming…she'll need to have a place to land after she's done there, and we made a deal. Coleen will come help me, and I'll help her as best I can."

"That's what family does for each other." She laughed and said it was what she did. "Yes, I can see that you're not like the rest of them. When she gets here, if she needs work, tell her to see one of my brothers. They're always looking for someone to come and help out. Especially out at the ranch with Joey and Chris."

After telling her again to call him if she needed anything, Tony made his way to his apartment. There were several messages on his service, all of which he decided could wait, and he looked at his emails. One of them was from Burke telling Tony that he had a house for him. Grabbing up his keys, he contacted him as he was headed to the address.

It's a done deal. Tony paused before starting his car. *I didn't do it. Myra did. And so you know, yes, it's almost furnished. She said it was harder to see what you wanted in a home, but what she did see, it's there.* He plugged in the address to the house and headed over.

Maybe I wanted to do this the old fashioned way. He told him good luck with that. *Yes, I'm beginning to see that having a very powerful witch in the family is going to take some getting used to.*

Yes. But you won't believe the things you can have done in your home. And Piper has a few of the faeries in the house too. Each of us have a few now to keep the house safe. I'm not sure what they can do that we can't as panthers, but you'll see them when you go over.

I'm headed there now. Please tell me it's not this giant fucking

house that I'm going to be wandering around in for the rest of my life.
He said he didn't know. *Why don't you meet me there? I'm almost
there now.*

As soon as he pulled into the gated driveway, he knew that
he was going to be looking at a house as big as his brothers',
when all he wanted was some land and a room to move into.
Pulling into the circular drive, he got out and stared. Christ,
the house looked like something that would be perfect on a
colonial movie set, complete with white pillars and rocking
chairs. He was going to murder Myra when he saw her.

Now Available in the
Bentley Legacy

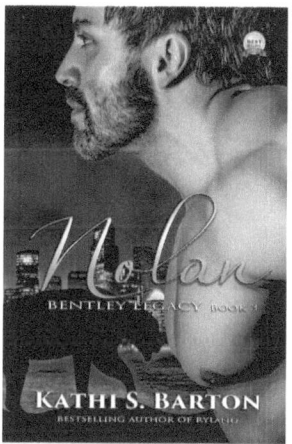

Before You Go…

HELP AN AUTHOR

write a review

THANK YOU!

Share your voice and help guide other readers to these wonderful books. Even if it's only a line or two your reviews help readers discover the author's books so they can continue creating stories that you'll love. Login to your favorite retailer and leave a review. Thank you.

AWARD WINNING, BESTSELLING AUTHOR

Kathi Barton, author of the bestselling series Force of Nature, lives in Nashport, Ohio with her husband Paul. In addition to writing full time Kathi likes to spend time with her eight grandkids, three children and three children-in-laws. She writes to relax and have fun.

Her muse, a cross between Jimmy Stewart and Hugh Jackman brings them to life for her readers in a way that has them coming back time and again for more. Her favorite genre is paranormal romance with a great deal of spice. You can visit Kathi on line and drop her an email if you'd like. She loves hearing from her fans. aaronskiss@gmail.com.

Follow Kathi on her blog: http://kathisbartonauthor.blogspot.com/

www.ingramcontent.com/pod-product-compliance
Lightning Source LLC
Chambersburg PA
CBHW032136170626
46808CB00006B/2262